Paula Burns is a Midland's based writer and artist. She trained as a psychoanalytic psychotherapist and worked for several years in the prison service and private practice in London, before taking early retirement due to a neurological illness. She has a background in Philosophy and Literature and was engaged in research at doctoral level at Warwick University. She lives with her husband, a fellow psychotherapist. Their extended family is composed of four children, six grandchildren and their cat Willow.

Paula's art and poetry can be viewed at www.paulaburns.co.uk

Blue-Grey Island

Paula Burns

Paula Burns

Matador
5 Weir Road
Kibworth Beauchamp
Leicester LE8 0LQ, UK
Tel: (+44) 116 279 2299
Email: books@troubador.co.uk
Web: www.troubador.co.uk/matador

This book is a work of fiction and, except in the case of historical figures
and minor factual details concerning their life histories, any resemblance
to actual persons, living or dead, is purely coincidental.

ISBN 978-1848762-565

A Cataloguing-in-Publication (CIP) catalogue record for this book
is available from the British Library.

Cover illustration © Eileen Harrisson

Typeset in 11pt Book Antiqua by Troubador Publishing Ltd, Leicester, UK
Printed in the UK by TJ International, Padstow, Cornwall

Matador is an imprint of Troubador Publishing Ltd

In loving memory of my father

Dedicated to Bernie

'Astronomy compels the soul to look upward, and leads us from this world to another'.

Plato, *The Republic*, 342 BC

'We do not ask for what useful purpose the birds do sing, for song is their pleasure since they were created for singing. Similarly, we ought not to ask why the human mind troubles to fathom the secrets of the heavens ... The diversity of the phenomena of Nature is so great, and the treasures hidden in the heavens so rich, precisely in order that the human mind shall never be lacking in fresh nourishment'.

Johannes Kepler, *'Mysterium Cosmographicum'*, 1596

Part One

Grange Farm

May 1987

Something frightening is happening to my mind.

I sense this for sure – in the way that you look at me – a certain anxiety betrayed by your eyes – a barely perceptible twitch at the corners of your mouth.

It has taken me ten minutes to write this. I could not remember how to spell 'perceptible'.

But sometimes, on days like this, I reach beyond the blur.

Mannie – I came up to the attic today and sat for a long time thinking.

'Nothing new in that!' you would say.

It is such a beautiful day, the sunshine freely given on a spring morning. I can see the orchard in the distance, the apple trees coming into blossom and even here, high up in the house, I am sure there is the hint of the sweet, pungent smell of bluebells.

I AM SURE?

How can I be sure of anything?

By tomorrow I may have forgotten that I wrote this and the effort it takes to put words together.

This is the start – the start of it all.

I am trying to work out now – while I still have some presence of mind – what it will be like to forget my past – what it will be like to forget my life – what it will be like to forget even you? I, who have spent so much time questioning the great imponderables, do not have an answer.

Often, I sit here watching the darkening horizon – waiting for the night sky to fill with stars. Oh – the wonder of the universe; to position my eye upon the lens of a telescope and search for God's signature in all that I see.

And this is not a belief that has been simply held. To love God and to love Science is not an easy path to tread – it has been a struggle. But you know all of this Mannie – you who have been my partner in life – the person who has witnessed these struggles.

In a moment I am going to squeeze some tubes of paint – the lovely squelch of the black and white, my fingers mixing the grey. I might add some Prussian blue.

And then the blur.

'To be a pioneer is only to lag behind the mind of the creator.'

Did I say that? I think I said it once – at a conference, or maybe I wrote it in a book

MY MIND IS DISINTEGRATING.

It is so hard to concentrate. Is there nothing left for me to do? Is there nothing but nothing?

Don't ever forget me Mannie – for I will surely forget myself. Did I ever really tell you how much I love and need you? You are my darling wife,

Ralph xx

July 1999

Water

R alph lies on his side, the side that faces the ward doors looking out onto a paved courtyard. It is a pretty courtyard, complete with raised beds, a small pond and a bench set in the shade. Sunlight bounces off the sandstone paving. The ward doors are open, in a futile attempt to freshen the stale air in the room.

'What a beautiful day,' a voice announces, brightly. 'July is such a lovely month. Just smell the scent coming off that lavender – I must take a cutting.'

A slight breeze wafts across the ward. Ralph has a cool sensation on his face. He is unable to describe the sensation with the word 'cool' but he moves his head around, like a relaxed cat about to wash, indicating he feels happy. Ralph has few words to describe his perceptions but he instinctively registers colours, shapes and sounds as existing outside of himself, as something 'other'.

Ralph looks out onto this other space of light and shade and mass. Sometimes, a piece of the mass breaks away, moves about, and this catches his attention. He is aware of a change in sensation as eye muscles tighten in an attempt to focus. One of the pieces is floating towards him; an exciting, white object that Ralph appears to recognise.

The exciting object has a name – Ruth. The name is written on a badge, neatly attached to her uniform. Ralph is unable to connect a name with a face – his vision is hazy and his mind befuddled – but he registers the timbre of Ruth's voice and his skin is sensitive to the reassuring touch of her hand.

Ruth holds the sprig of lavender to Ralph's nose, as she encourages him to sit up. 'Smell this my darling, isn't it just too lovely?'

The voice has a familiar Geordie accent but Ralph doesn't recognise it as such. There is a stirring within his mind akin to a lightning bolt. This is how it is for Ralph when a brain synapse, connected to memory, suddenly fires into life.

'W ... water' he stutters, jerking his head as he struggles to enunciate.

'You want a drink, how about a nice cup of tea?' Ruth suggests, withdrawing the sprig of lavender.

Ralph is agitated. 'W ... water!' he cries, ringing his hands and shaking his body to and fro.

But Ruth is walking away, with the key to Ralph's memory of a heather strewn moor and the soft, northern lilt of a sweetheart whose voice he had once likened to a gently flowing stream.

Opera

Ruth eventually returns, holding the offending cup of tea. Cups of tea are a marker of time on Ward B; as are meals, bed baths, the dispensing of medication and doctors' rounds.

Ralph has no clear notion of time but he understands the difference between proximity and distance. He feels enveloped by a calming presence when Ruth is near to him because she has an aura of serenity. Often, he is simply aware of a white, diffuse light when she is tending to his needs, and time is experienced as the anxious space that opens up in the gap between the light's appearance and disappearance.

Today, Margaret is on duty with Ruth. Margaret is experienced as a rough-edged, scratchy white object by Ralph – an object he distinguishes by a loud clacking noise, which suddenly invades the atmosphere around him. The object moves at high velocity and is perceived by Ralph as a violently flashing zigzag of white light.

Margaret is one of the nurses who feels that Ruth mollycoddles her patients, and that the making of cups of tea should be left to the auxiliary staff.

Ruth holds back as she observes that Margaret is about to change Ralph's bed. The sudden swish of curtains is a hurricane of air to his sensitive ears. Basic tasks: the change of incontinence pad, and the provision of clean bedding and pyjamas are methodically executed. The curtains are hurriedly re-drawn and Ralph is left turning his head from side-to-side whilst feverishly clutching at his pyjama jacket. Ruth waits for Margaret to vacate the scene before walking over to Ralph with her steady pace.

'Calm down, little man,' she gently urges, stroking his head, 'what in heaven's name has upset you?'

Ralph relaxes as a sensation of softness sweeps across the space that we know to be his face.

'Today is a happy day,' Ruth continues, as she settles Ralph against his pillows and pours the tea into a drinking beaker, 'because Mannie is coming to see you. Now we want you to be looking your best for your wife.'

'Mannie.' Ralph repeats the word with a sense of satisfaction and then continues with an expression of confusion. 'Mannie – no … but … m … mu … mummy!'

Now he is chuckling, shaking with laughter.

'Oh Ralph,' Ruth sighs, taking hold of his hand, 'you are such a one. I tried reading your book again last night but I couldn't understand a word of it. All I know about the stars is from reading the daily horoscope! You know, you are a very clever man.'

Ruth scans the ward, deliberating who needs her attention. She is reluctant to leave Ralph but knows that his wife will arrive promptly at visiting time. Amy, a fragile octogenarian, has just woken and is shuffling in her chair attempting to reach a drinking beaker. Ruth notes the signs of 'half-life' emanating from her patients – the laboured breathing and intermittent snoring that provides a perpetual acoustic backdrop to her daily work.

The sonic boom of a low flying aircraft magnifies and echoes in the heat, causing the patients to stir and cry out in confusion. The commotion galvanizes Ruth into action.

'It's all right Amy, let me fetch your beaker – I'm coming over right now,' she calls across the ward, whilst gently squeezing Ralph's hand. 'You just rest quietly my dear, Mannie will be here any minute.'

A large clock dominates Ward B – the sound of its ticking gets into Ralph's brain. The tick, tick, tick meets with a rhythm that enforces a swaying movement throughout his body. The rhythm acts as a magnetic force directing energy across the ward. A unified swaying and rocking has taken over from the stillness.

Margaret is in a tetchy mood; the continual rocking is getting on her nerves. 'Stop that Ralph,' she complains, 'you've managed to set the whole ward off!'

Ralph just rocks the harder as he babbles in Amy's direction.

'Baby,' Amy inexplicably cries, in a high-pitched tone, 'baby … baby.'

'I think you're the baby,' Margaret retorts, half amused. 'Who had to be changed twice this morning – huh?'

Tick, tick, tick … no – slower, tick, tick … tick, tick … tick, tick ….

The ticking lulls Ralph's mind and senses into a state of pre-verbal bliss. He is safe in his mother's womb, her heartbeat amplified by the rush of blood and the warm lapping of embryonic waters.

'Baby … baby … baby!' Amy continues to cry.

Ralph breaks into song. 'Ave Ma … Maria,' he croons.

11

Margaret presses a hand to her damp forehead. The air in the room is diminishing; damn the porter for not replacing the broken fan and trust Ralph to start a wave of pandemonium.

Ruth walks across the floor towards a figure that has just entered the ward. The figure is dressed in pastel pink and embraces Ruth. In Ralph's world he is aware of a contrast in colour as the white and pink objects merge – becoming one – and then separate.

'Hello there, how are you are?' Ruth greets Mannie affectionately. 'Come and see what we have today. Your dearest is entertaining us with Ave Maria. Do you know the next bit; he gets stuck after the first two words?'

Mannie hurries over. The sight of her husband singing is heartening in comparison to her last visit, when he had cried and rocked all afternoon.

'That was his mother's favourite piece,' Mannie informs Ruth as the two women gather round the bed. 'She had a wonderful voice, you know. She reckoned Ralph came into the world knowing all the major liturgical and operatic works.'

'Baby ... baby ... baby!' Amy cries louder.

Margaret raises her eyes to the ceiling. 'Its just one of those afternoons,' she sighs, and then more magnanimously, 'It's the heat making them fractious. Would you like a cold drink Mannie? Now Amy – will you please pipe down.'

Opium

Mannie stands before Ralph in her pastel pink dress. It is made from mixed fibres and doesn't breathe – she is in a sweat.

The dress had been chosen in the usual desultory manner, running her fingers along the coat hangers in the wardrobe. Pastel pinks, sky blues, lemons. The garments hang limp, in colour-coded columns that have been sorted with great precision.

This precision is not a natural aspect of Mannie's nature. The ability to systematically organise every item in the house grew out of necessity as her husband's illness progressed.

'Hello, my darling,' Mannie whispers, moving close to Ralph's ear and taking his shaking hands in her own. 'You have cold hands, cold hands on such a hot day.'

Ralph experiences a tickling sensation in his nose as his sense of smell is alerted to a heavy fragrance.

Mannie has daubed Opium perfume behind her ears, on her wrists and, for good measure, across her breastbone. She dislikes the smell; it is far too heady and makes her feel nauseous. Familiarity, the doctors had stressed, keep up the familiarity.

The perfume had been a present from their daughter

Sophia, many Christmases ago. Ralph laughed after Sophia left.

'Phew – that's a bit on the heavy side. I wouldn't wear it unless you've got me around for protection!'

But the laughter metamorphosed into deep kisses and Ralph made love to her with a passion Mannie thought had long diminished. This had been the start of her resolution to 'try harder'. The perfume became an emblem of Mannie's wavering resolve. It sat on the dressing table, gathering dust, a reminder of her ambivalence.

Mannie is not one for keeping up with the times. She hasn't quite progressed beyond the fashion statements of the fifties, arguing with Sophia that you had to have been stung by the fashion bug in the sixties to get on the bandwagon of ever-changing fads.

Sophia had pleaded with her mother to update her wardrobe; to cut her long mousy hair into a chic bob. Mannie likes her long hair, highlighting out the odd grey strand has been her one concession to vanity. Now she wears it hastily pulled back into a flimsy chignon. As for her love life, Ralph and she had enjoyed a comfortable relationship up until the illness. Their lovemaking had been warm and familiar, if infrequent. They were the best of friends. But that expression of passion, it reminded her of how things had been at the beginning. If Mannie were honest, it haunted her.

Ralph's hand breaks free of Mannie's. His fingers pull at the pastel pink dress. He feels a sensation of energy draining away. There is a contracting and aching that is inextricably connected to looking at the fuzzy, pink mass.

Mannie's lips move. Ralph is mesmerised by the opening

and closing of this cavernous space. It is all mixed in with his sense of absence and presence. Instinctively, he leans over, pressing his mouth onto the opening – then pulls back with surprise. Mannie's lips are the sting of the awareness of 'other'. The contracting ache grows stronger as Ralph leans over again. He feels like he is falling. Swooning, swirling, his body has the lightness of a leaf spiralling down from a tall tree. His lips on Mannie's, flesh on flesh – the heady, instinctive memory of a first kiss.

The China Pot

Mannie isn't sure which is worse, day or night.

At night, she places pillows down one side of the bed, Ralph's side, and drapes an old shirt over the pillow next to her head. The shirt smells of Ralph, a mixture of warm, soapy spices. Ralph's shaving kit is still in the bathroom. Each morning Mannie removes the lid from the wooden shaving bowl and puts her nose close to the block of soap. She remembers the intimacy of the bathroom, how Ralph and she would talk, losing track of time, as the water in the bathtub went lukewarm and eventually cold.

Mannie buries her face in Ralph's shirt and gives way to tears. The tears flow without censure. She rarely allows herself this release during the day.

Daybreak. Mannie rubs her eyes and reaches out to the bedside table for a small china pot. The pot was once her mother's; it had sat for years on the triple-mirrored dressing table in her parents' bedroom. Mannie has fond memories of Netta and Ronald Parks – particularly her father's good humour. 'Fifty years of wedded bliss,' he would joke with a conspiratorial wink in her mother's direction. Mannie held onto the template of her parents' relationship as a reference point, whenever she felt herself failing according to some self-imposed mythical standard of a 'good' marriage.

There are delicate hand-painted roses round the edge of the pot reminding Mannie of the whimsy of a bygone age. Her fingers dig deep, searching for some foam earplugs.

The dawn chorus is distracting. The first sensation Mannie has when she wakes is one of grief; it is mixed in with birdsong and she can't stand it.

'Listen to the birds,' Ralph laughed joyously, on their first morning together.

Mannie had sat up in bed, suddenly remembering where she was (the Northumberland Moors) and with whom (Ralph Drew – the shy junior lecturer from the Physic's department, who had a passion for Cosmology and Astronomy).

Then she lay back on the pillows, white damask pillows that were dappled with sunlight, and smiled at Ralph. He had courted her with a sensitivity bordering on reticence, and here they were four months later – lovers.

'Pull back the lace curtains,' she suggested, even though she was holding Ralph close to her.

Ralph sat up, stretching an arm towards the window as Mannie gently ran her fingers down his back. A strange sense of possessiveness settled within Mannie's mind. Ralph's flesh was now connected with her own and whatever awareness she had of her own skin was utterly transformed by this connection.

'It is beautiful, splendid!' Ralph murmured, as he looked out onto the Northumberland countryside. 'I want to stay here forever.'

Daybreak. Mannie attempts to sleep some more. This is the time of day she calls her 'waking sleep' – when dreams are so vivid it takes the entire morning to reach consciousness. Every time Mannie reaches for the china pot she thinks of her mother and this image invariably sets off a spiral of dreams. Netta is a dumpy little figure with tightly permed grey hair and laughing eyes.

'Now Hinny, when one door shuts another door opens.'

Her mother is full of proverbs; they are woven together into a tight fabric, out of which she has made a security blanket to be grasped for comfort in any worrying situation. It takes Mannie until lunchtime to comprehend, in a way that seems real, that her mother is dead. Ralph sometimes asks for Netta but Mannie cannot figure why this is so when he can no longer recollect the name of their daughter.

Mannie is afraid of these ramblings, having read that in the last stages of delirium, before death, a person seeks out the dead in order to make reconciliations. But Ralph had never been estranged from Netta so she tries to convince herself that the situation might improve – rationalising that the delirium has been caused by the fall and is different to the dementia. Mannie clings to the belief that there is a route out of delirium marked 'improvement', which is not the case with dementia, a condition that inevitably worsens.

'I am fooling myself, aren't I?' she had said to Ruth on her last visit, but Ruth merely smiled and replied with optimism, 'Well you never know, if we can get the infection under control he might improve.'

Mannie realises this is well-intentioned kindness but she needs someone to be straight with her. What she really requires is for someone to be brave enough to say, 'Ralph is dying – go home and prepare for the inevitable.'

Ralph is agitated by the kiss. He holds the top of his head and rocks. Amy becomes alert; she watches the proceedings now with the studied attention of a frightened bird. Her head cocks on one side, her crooked elbows flap with quivering wing-like movements. She is preparing for flight.

Mannie re-positions her chair in order to avoid facing Amy. There is some kind of connection between Ralph and this withered old lady that irritates her. Amy cackles excitedly and scrutinizes as Mannie reaches into her shopping bag. The bag is made from shiny PVC and printed with a William Morris design. Mannie produces a photograph album and leans nearer to the edge of the bed, ready to begin, yet again, the story of Ralph's family history. She is tempted to begin with the final pages of the album – the photos of Sophia from babyhood to adulthood.

'Ralph, did I tell you, Sophia is coming to stay the weekend? It means I'll be able to come again on Sunday because she'll drive me here.'

Ralph pulls at the pages of the album.

'Ah!' he cries out, so that Amy jumps, startled from her watchful position, knocking her drinking beaker to the floor. To Ralph, it is all a fluttering of wings now, as Margaret struts across the floor to retrieve the beaker.

Ralph moans. The increase of sensory stimulation sends him into overload. He feels overwhelmed by a flapping of white and pink feathers. Amy continues to shuffle noisily on her black vinyl chair – its non-porous surface sticks to her skin in the heat. A knitted grey cardigan engulfs her tiny frame and she waves her arms about, in a struggle to release her hands from the elongated, itchy wool sleeves.

Ralph attempts to make sense of all the distorted

sounds and movement, and within this moment he perceives Amy as a small, grey bird – perched on a rocky outpost, trembling with fear.

Cholinergic Neurons

When Ralph was first diagnosed with vascular dementia and then early onset Alzheimer's he demanded to see the space inside of his head that was 'letting him down'.

Apparently the two conditions were a devastating brew – vascular dementia involving a slow and conscious evacuation of the ability to function as normal and Alzheimer's a much swifter and less conscious forgetting of all one once knew of self and nearest and dearest.

Ralph's request was not simple. As a scientist he felt compelled to visualise the evidence and politely demanded to see the site of his brain cells exploding into nothingness. He preferred this image of explosion, all hot fizz and sparking, to the notion of a cell simply dying – in rather a limp way. Ralph had studied the latest research – learning that the crucial nerve cells, cholinergic neurons, could be coaxed to stay alive when supplied with a brain chemical called nerve growth factor. He reluctantly acknowledged that the research was primarily being done on monkeys and that there was no chance of a major breakthrough in his lifetime.

The MRI scan had been rather disappointing. Ralph scrutinised the bluish-grey area that signified the burial site of his once healthy brain cells and felt that it was just too ... well ... grey.

Mannie was sitting next to him, silent and strained. He sensed that she was willing him to ask the consultant 'how long?' Ralph resisted asking such a definitive question. He was used to thinking of the notion of time as wedded to the infinity of space. Within a pinprick of time, that signified his life and a sense of consciousness, his realisation of self would be extinguished.

Ralph's mind meandered. What if space and time weren't infinite? Some would argue that space was finite yet unbounded. But even so – there was no time without space, and as the body existed in space so the body existed in time. What happened to the soul at death? Did it slip through a veil to a non-material space, meaning it was no longer positioned inside of time – constrained by time? If this were possible one could deduce that the soul was pure energy, unlike the body.

And, he mused, did all this mean that God, or at least some higher creative impulse, potentially existed outside of space and time, and had by some stupendous feat created the spark that had ignited the beginnings of the universe? Could such a position be argued for?

Ralph's head hurt. He had abandoned this process of thinking so long ago – tired of the endless argumentation – the logical proofs for the existence of God and the semantics against; the whole cosmological roller-coaster of proof and negation. Surely he had decided decades ago that there was no concrete proof for God's existence; just a sense of connection with a higher power – if that was the route one's faith or inclination took? But the route inevitably cut straight through a secular world, where religious conflict (based on the 'unholy trinity' of politics, religious dogma and the tyrannical imposition of power) was played out.

Ralph sensed Mannie's gaze upon him – she was keenly attuned to his mind's wanderings. He knew that Mannie would need to come to terms with the situation in her own way. Mannie would fret about how to use the time left, how to make up for lost time.

Had he and Mannie lost time, he asked himself? Possibly, and some of what they had lost, the memory of it, already lay dead within the blue-grey mass that he was looking at, lit up on the wall in the consultant's room.

Ralph had been drawn to 'looking' beyond the surface appearance of objects from being a young boy.

'It all started on my tenth birthday,' he had explained to Mannie. 'It was the best present I'd ever been given.'

Mannie thinks about this statement whenever she walks over to Ralph's desk in the attic and picks up the microscope that he had been given as a child.

The present acted as a catalyst for Ralph's fascination with 'another world' that is invisible to the naked eye. Playmates gathered round with offerings to be scrutinised: the leg of a spider, a freshly picked scab, a strand of hair, but Ralph harboured more romantic notions. He had seen pictures of the structure of a snowflake and was mesmerised by its delicacy, by the fact that no two snowflakes were the same. He waited all winter for it to snow, his nose pressed against the cold glass of his bedroom window. It didn't snow that winter but Ralph held the 'information' close to his heart. Nothing was as it seemed on the surface. This was surely a profound state of affairs? Ralph felt that the secret of the universe had unveiled itself before his child's eyes.

It was with these eyes that Ralph viewed the MRI scan.

There had to be more to it than could be easily seen. He wanted to magnify every single brain cell, even if his brain chemistry functioned as a corporate network. He visualised each cell with the intensity of his childhood imagination, out of the same necessity.

'Most things are too big to place under a microscope,' he had told his teacher Miss Phipps, who took a kindly interest in him as a young boy.

'I suppose they are,' she had replied. 'But science is geared to finding a way of looking at objects no matter what their size or distance.'

Ralph thought about this; he was chewing over a problem. In his child's mind he hadn't quite figured out the difference between a microscope and a telescope. Perhaps the difficulty was that scientists were trying to look at large objects too close up; and then there was the problem of how to bring distant objects close enough to explore in detail.

He puzzled for a while on the problem of perspective. What of the moon and stars? The moon appeared as a dinner plate hung low in the sky; as for the stars, they were tiny, twinkling objects no bigger than his fingernail. An image of a huge elephant, suspended in distant space, popped into his mind. He first thought of viewing the creature just a few yards away. But what if the elephant was placed on the moon – how large would it be? The elephant looked bigger than the moon, but positioned at such a distance it might become a tiny dot on its cratered surface.

If the elephant was a long way off it could be viewed in its entirety, by means of a special instrument. Ralph held an imaginary instrument to his eye, pretending to capture the creature as it stood on the surface of the moon. Yes, here was the elephant's leathery hide, criss-crossed with a multitude of pathways, along which marched armies of tiny millipedes. Ralph was certain that his imaginary instrument would answer all of his questions. He did not tell Miss Phipps of his discovery, but he often repeated the details of the story to Mannie, roaring with laughter.

'Of course,' he recalled, 'dear Miss Phipps enlightened me. A couple of days later she sat me down with an encyclopaedia. "Look at this Ralph," she implored – her eyebrows rising above the rim of her spectacles like two birds flying on the horizon. "In 1608 an instrument called the spyglass was invented."

I was entranced and repeated the word spyglass like an excited parrot. Then Miss Phipps pointed to some text. "See here Ralph, it says – *a certain instrument for seeing far... a device for seeing things at a distance as if they were near.*"

Well, she explained a little about Galileo – how he had begun with the obvious uses of a spyglass, which were maritime and terrestrial observations, but rapidly moved on to astronomy. So Mannie, in my child's mind I had been grappling with one of the burning questions intriguing Galileo – how to see beyond what meets the human eye? There is not a fundamental question about the universe that a five year old has not puzzled on.'

Mannie was not sure about this. She thought perhaps Ralph had been an exceptional child but that any precociousness, that might have become arrogance in later life, was tempered by his determination to always put God into the equation. Mannie felt it was inevitable that Ralph had not become your wholly materialist sort of scientist. He had a romantic nature that seemed able to peacefully co-exist with a healthy scepticism and deeply enquiring mind. This 'peace' had not been easily won.

Ralph's mind had matured within an era during which the cosmological map was continually redrawn to the point where God was apportioned an ambiguous role in the creation of the universe. It was not the ever-changing detail that bothered Ralph but how the acquisition of new knowledge might be received. Could he retain his state of wonderment (a legacy from childhood), and his belief in an elemental force behind the mysteries of the cosmos (a legacy from his Catholic upbringing)? All of the particulars of Ralph's life story were played out against this backdrop of tension between Science and religious belief and his deep need for harmony on the subject.

Ralph had continued to work on the possibilities for the composition of dark matter, which makes up twenty-five percent of the invisible mass of the Galaxy, since he had taken early retirement. Most of his research was at the 'thinking' level, since his removal from the world of high-tech. Ralph the romanticist had taken over from Ralph the observer and scientist.

Before the diagnosis Mannie had harboured dreams of their buying a Winnebago, in which to head for the mountainous terrain of North America, no doubt calling in on some astronomy institute. Ralph had travelled quite a bit in his younger days, giving lectures on Cosmology and Astronomy and despite his shy nature people warmed to him. There were good friends to visit and Mannie felt this would make a contrast to their rather secluded and self-contained existence. But Ralph had simply headed for the attic, inhabiting the uppermost space of their tumbledown house; a space that had always functioned as a kind of observatory-cum-office. He referred to his activities as 'Science as reverie'.

Mannie climbs the wooden staircase to the attic daily, with her morning cup of tea. The stairs tire her – one flight to the first landing, another flight to the second floor and then the steep ascent to the attic. The attic is freezing in winter then stuffy in summer. The first thing she does on these hot summer mornings is to open a casement window, closing her eyes in hopeful anticipation of a cooling breeze. When Mannie re-opens her eyes she is reluctant to linger on the magnificent view; the luminescent glow of sunlight on green-golden fields and the spire of a church, almost hidden by the foliage of trees, as it nestles in the valley – because this vista is inextricably connected to a memory.

'This has to be it,' Ralph had spoken after they had clambered up a rickety ladder and across gaping floorboards.

They had stood mesmerised by the view and Ralph had felt himself swoon, his eyes drawn towards a landscape that seemed to stretch towards infinity, filled with nothing but beauty. Ralph had an eye for the future. Despite his involvement with scientific research he knew that progress was a mixed bag. Not all change was for good. The farmhouse was a protected space: no traffic, no factories, and – most importantly – no manufactured light polluting the night skies.

'It is lovely,' Mannie ventured, 'but it needs so much work. How will we manage Ralph?'

'We have our whole lives in front of us Mannie. Imagine bringing up a family here. We can just work at it at our own pace.'

Ralph looked out, once again, over the lush landscape.

'We can sit here and watch the sun go down. I think I shall want to paint. See how the light keeps changing, pink to lilac to golden yellow. It's wonderful!'

Grey was not a colour that interested Ralph at this time. Grey was for the future.

Elm Cottage
April 14th - 1940

Dear Mrs Drew,

Thank you so much for your kind letter concerning Ralph's scholarship.

I am thrilled that Ralph will be continuing his education and this is surely down to his own hard work and determination as much as anything I have done. Also, he does of course have the support of a wonderful mother!

I will never forget when Ralph first came to my attention, a rather shy and fragile young boy of eight who would approach me at the end of class and tentatively ask the most interesting questions. I like to think that the telescope we awarded Ralph for the school year prize (to compliment his nascent fascination with all things microscopic!) helped him on his way. He was just eleven at the time.

As you know I will soon be retiring. During my years of teaching I have taken an interest in many of my pupils but none stand out in my mind in quite the way Ralph does.

Your son is unique, not least because his intellect combines with a gentle temperament. So many individuals think they need brute force and arrogance to get ahead in life, made worse by these troubled times we live in. I am confident that Ralph will prove them wrong. I feel he is destined for a great future.

My very best wishes to you and your family,

Agnes Phipps

Painting

When Ralph first saw the MRI scan he immediately began to experience it as a painting. Part of the painting pulsated with luminous reds, greens and yellows; a swirling sea that splashed around the edges of the blue-grey mass. Ralph focused hard on the dark mass and tried to imagine what it might represent. He decided that it was an island, a blue-grey flint stoned island, a wild and uninhabited terrain. He felt that part of him already inhabited this space and that another part of him was being propelled towards it. The latter was a reluctant explorer, filled with fear and dread. He had no choice, the island beckoned – was calling him with the force of a mythological Siren. But this was no sweet, seductive song; it was the crazy, undulating force of madness.

Mannie sits by the attic window attempting to get her breath back. It is all part of her morning routine: waking at day break, putting her earplugs in, dreaming fitfully, rising late in a confused state, then making a cup of tea before climbing flights of stairs to the remnants of Ralph's inner world.

The attic walls are covered by Ralph's paintings. The paintings span five years, from 1987, when the illness was first diagnosed, until 1992. After that point Ralph lost his ability to paint, lost the ability to convey what was happening for him in any meaningful way. Ralph might disagree with this judgement; it is a point of view that is positioned from beyond his island terrain. He is in the thick of it now, deep within the centre where the blue-grey mass bleeds into black.

Mannie gets her breath back and moves to the large pine desk at the far end of the attic. Each time she does this she has the same memory, the recollection of Ralph making the desk in the attic because he knew he wouldn't get the size he wanted through the trap door. Ralph was no carpenter and Mannie had praised his efforts in the way one would a small child. She did this with no sense of derision but by way of making amends. Ralph had experienced little praise as a child from his father. It was a source of wonder to Mannie that her husband's intellect had survived his background at all.

Background? Ralph had questioned the genetic links concerning his illness. The consultant assured him that there was no definite evidence to prove that Alzheimer's was inherited. Mannie thought this was more out of deference to their having a child, as no one wanted to feel they might pass on an incurable condition to the next generation. Ralph thought quietly to himself that it was probably only a matter of time before a gene for Alzheimer's was discovered. Thinking back, to his father's death, Ralph was forced to bypass the comforting words. His father had undertaken a strange passage from his usual black moods to a new form of craziness in his late fifties. His mother had put it down to the drink. 'Decades of self abuse,' she would sadly announce, without any hint of the anger one would expect. Ralph thought about his father's increased aggression, his demise in an institution. It had been hard to feel sympathy because his father had led his mother a harsh life. But it made Ralph go cold inside, the memory of this burly man reduced to a quivering whippet; skin and bone, slobber and nonsense.

As Ralph's illness progressed an unfamiliar sense of isolation clouded his mind. He began to wish there was someone in his family he could have a conversation with, but he had no siblings and his parents were dead. His family tree began post 1919, when his mother Camille Dupont had married Thomas Drew. Thomas had fallen for the pretty Red Cross nurse, 'his angel in blue and white', who had attended to him in France, as he lay seriously ill with an injury inflicted by 'Jerry'. Ralph knew only a few details of his mother's past before this event.

Admittedly, his great-grandmother's name, Marie Dupont, and his grandmother Catherine, had been mentioned on a couple of occasions, but Ralph had realised, from a young age, that his mother was estranged from her birth family. Her reticence had discouraged any curiosity he might have had in tracing their family history.

After the diagnosis he found himself grasping for the DNA of his ancestors. Images of double stranded helixes floated around in his imagination. He began to paint the snake- like apparitions, placing them in suspension within an aqueous cobalt-blue solution.

Ralph felt that he was swimming in the solution; he sensed himself energetically twirling around the strands of DNA and the more he twirled the more he believed that he was creating an indestructible part of himself, a part that lay beyond the clutches of faulty gene structures.

'Blue,' he quietly murmured to Mannie, 'blue is the colour of the imagination.'

The Bridge at Courbevoie

Mannie attempts to calm Ralph. She is relieved that Margaret is attending to Amy, suggesting that she might like to take a turn in the courtyard garden. Mannie gently removes the photo album from Ralph's twitching fingers.

'Let's start at the beginning Ralph, just as we always do.'

Ralph's vision struggles to fix on a postcard that has been pasted onto the first page of the album. He senses colour and shifting shape, as blurred swirling dots dance before his eyes. A rippling sensation pulls at his scalp. The sensation causes Ralph to become more agitated. He feels the tug of loss of memory; his skin prickles and his head hurts.

'Do you remember the postcard Ralph? Sophia bought it for you – well lots of postcards – because you like the painting so much.'

Ralph stares at Mannie – not comprehending.

Mannie is persistent, despite her knowing that Ralph's vision is clouded. She feels that she must keep trying – that to give up would be to give up on Ralph completely.

'Look Ralph – it is a postcard of one of your favourite paintings; *The Bridge at Courbevoie*.' Mannie speaks hesitantly, suddenly unsure of her pronunciation.

She gives a little chuckle as she looks round the ward.

As though anyone here is going to tick her off about her French! But this is Mannie; a little naive, somewhat reticent and uncertain.

A larger print of the painting hangs on the wall in Mannie's sitting room. Ralph had developed an obsessive attachment to the painting during the latter years of the illness. He had taken the print down from the wall, insisting on carrying it with him wherever he went. Sometimes he stabbed at the surface of the print with the tips of his fingers.

A numbing weariness descended upon Mannie during this period. The print was too cumbersome; it was becoming a problem for her trying to attend to Ralph's needs, keeping him clean, feeding him, settling him down at night, always with the picture in tow.

'Do you remember Ralph, the day Sophia arrived with a dozen postcards of this print?' she chuckles once again. 'We pasted the postcards all over the house, so that you would never be apart from the picture.'

Mannie looks at the picture. She knows why Ralph originally admired it. The painting, with its gently sloping riverbank and wooden boardwalks, from which a solitary angler fishes, evokes a sense of repose and calm stability. The still surface of the water reflects the bridge in the distance and the unfurled sail of a small boat positioned in the foreground. The hazy mist and the subtle play of light on the water are captured by Seurat's distinct style of painting – myriad dots of complementary colours that fall upon the retina of the eye to be mixed and interpreted by the visual cortex. But Ralph's vision can no longer select and mix the splashes of violets and yellowish greens into the colours and form of a river landscape.

For Mannie, the picture is a reminder of a treasured holiday she and Ralph had enjoyed many years ago. They had rented a cottage on the outskirts of Paris – visiting Courbevoie several times during their stay. Ralph had enthused about Seurat, his innovative use of colour theory and expressed how sad it was that the gifted artist had died young.

Ralph can no longer explain why the painting became so meaningful for him. It was all to do with a notion, held at the beginning of his illness, that Seurat would have been able to paint the interiority of Ralph's mind – and that this painting would not have contained the colour grey in a life-draining state but would have simply intimated an area of darker shadow.

Part Two

Paris 1886

Chevreul's Birthday Party

Michel Eugène Chevreul, one time director of dyes at Gobelins textile factory, has given some thought to the artistic expression of the colour grey. He would have empathy for Ralph's aesthetic response to the MRI scan.

The year is 1886 and it is a bright August morning. Paris is buzzing with excitement in anticipation of a grand party. Marie Dupont has endured an unsettled night – in anticipation of a different event. The previous evening she had begged her mother to fetch the local midwife. Madame Dupont had tut-tutted and fretted; her hands plunged in a doughy mixture. She was busy baking. Many of the women of Paris were locked in this pose, stood over a scrubbed wooden table, set out with eggs, flour and fat, all ready to bake cakes for a day of national celebration.

'Well my daughter, you are about to discover what it is to be a woman and why I was so angry when you told me about the child!' Madame Dupont's ample fingers had worked the dough with frenzy, sending clouds of flour into the air.

The 'child' had been turning somersaults within the confined space of Marie's womb for the past month. She held her swollen stomach, with pudgy fingers not dissimilar to her mother's, and mimicked the kneading movement. Marie is but fourteen and words such as *womb*, *vagina*, *placenta*, *labour*, are woefully absent from her vocabulary. Scarcely more than a child herself, and a little on the slow side, she expects the baby to arrive with the ease of pulling a doll from the baggy sleeve of her mother's coat. This simple act is how Madame Dupont has endeavoured to teach her daughter the principles of the last stage of labour.

Marie had given her mother a look of unstudied insolence. It seems to Madame Dupont that her daughter has always looked this way, simply can't help herself. *He* could not have been taken with her daughter's looks, she surmises, whenever she thinks about Henri Moret. Henri Moret, the local butcher, denied all knowledge of the child. Well that was typical; the name of Dupont would last forever because none of the women ever seemed to get married. It had been Madame Dupont's misfortune to have an illegitimate child and now here was history repeating itself.

Madame Dupont had taken leave of her baking to fetch Berthe Rouart, the self-assigned midwife. She had noted the time. It was 7·30pm and if she were lucky Berthe would not be in a drink-sodden state. But then, she surmised, with the party the next day, her friend may have begun celebrating already.

The clock has gone full circle and sunlight streaks across the florid face of Berthe as she sleeps slumped in a chair, next to Marie's bed. She had wanted to take leave of the Dupont household the night before, having already been dragged away from a carousel at her lodgings.

Such nonsense, she sighed, these young girls seemed to have no notion that their frolics would result in misery. As for the Church, what did it care with its stories of limbo, hell and damnation? Limbo was life on the streets – she should know! Marie Dupont had been sent to her for 'an intervention', a few months ago, but it was too late. The child she was carrying would have to be born.

'It is not time yet,' Berthe had announced, from beneath a canopy of petticoats and sheets, after being summoned to Marie – who petulantly refused to undress.

'It must be time,' Marie had whimpered, accusingly. 'I can feel a tugging, the baby don't want to stay inside any longer.'

'Hours yet!' Berthe insisted, 'I can come back in the morning.'

Madame Dupont smelt the absinthe on Berthe's breath; more of the intoxicating liquor had seemed the only way to make her stay.

Chevreul is also caught in a shaft of sunlight as he kneels, on arthritic knees, at prayer. He is thanking God for his long life; for today is his hundredth birthday and the entire nation are preparing to celebrate the fact. This is the point in time where Ralph needs to dip into the gene pool. Chevreul is at prayer, waiting for Madame Dupont to come and assist him. She arrives; Chevreul can hear her now, the clatter of shoes on the staircase as she races up to his rooms at the Museum. The door is flung open.

'Oh Monsieur Chevreul, such a to-do!'

Chevreul looks up in anticipation. Madame Dupont stands before him, her face ruddy from running and her bonnet askew. She is in a worse state of dishevelment than usual.

'What is it Madame – you seem in some distress?'

Chevreul addresses his visitor with a formality that belies their relaxed relationship.

'It is Marie,' Madame Dupont wheezes, collapsing onto a chair. 'She says that the baby is coming, but I have had to leave her with Berthe Rouart ....' The voice trails off to a whisper with the mention of Berthe's name.

Chevreul frowns. He does not approve of Berthe. It was in order to rescue Madame Dupont and her daughter from such company that he had offered the kindness of employment. This act had been a wholly philanthropic gesture.

Chevreul is a remarkable individual. He first spied Madame Dupont ten years ago, selling cheese at the local market. Even then he was sprightly, despite his ninety years. It was a rare occurrence for Chevreul to be out walking, in this casual way. Normally, every physical and mental effort was geared to one purpose – intellectual achievement; his strict routine to work at his desk all day, every day, only ever leaving the seclusion of his rooms to attend scientific meetings. Why did this woman attract his attention, one among many, strained with the cares of life, her youth drawn out of her like sap seeping out from a cut on a young tree? Maybe it was the child he first saw, with her insolent dark eyes and tangle of bright curls.

Something occurred within Chevreul's mind to make him linger on this vignette of mother and child. Perhaps a flashback to his own family, his days of married life or 'day of married life' as his wife had joked. She had tolerated her husband's devotion to his work with good humour. Chevreul only visited his home on a Saturday evening, stopping over until Sunday when he would return to his rooms at the Museum. That was another lifetime, for Chevreul had been blessed with several. His wife was long dead and his son grown up. The old master had lived a life of seclusion for over twenty years, assisted by two elderly servants.

Chevreul made an instinctive decision to help the woman and child with an offer of care and financial maintenance in exchange for domestic help. Elise Dupont, the lowly daughter of a local farmer, who had disgraced the family with an illegitimate child, became Madame Dupont, the assistant and friend of the revered Michel Eugène Chevreul. No one could understand the situation, least of all the faithful servants who had quietly worked their way round their master for years. There was little for Madame Dupont to do, they argued, other than small amounts of cooking (she did know how to bake pastries, they conceded) and a little washing and mending. It was a blessing, they concluded, that her visits were sporadic and normally to the main house, not the revered rooms at the museum. Chevreul always found work for the obnoxious woman, putting up with her idle chatter. It was all a mystery, the servants grumbled. No reason could be divined other than the master wanting to make a charitable gesture before he left the world.

Elise had not expected her good fortune to last; Chevreul was so very old and could surely die at any time. But her employer was not focussed on dying – not while he still felt he had important work to do.

Theories

Ralph is not so fortunate. Death is a dark-winged bird that inhabits Blue-Grey Island. The creature is larger than an eagle, its wingspan casting a menacing shadow over the rocky crags upon which it perches. The bird sits and watches; it has eyes of flame and a hooked red beak.

Mannie grew accustomed to the creature as it appeared on a regular basis in Ralph's sketches. The early pictures were dense with colour and detail. Ralph methodically applied dots and lines, blunting the watercolour pencils, which he threw across the room for Mannie to sharpen. It seemed to give him some sense of ease, this process of drawing. It was as though he exerted control over the creature whilst involved in the act of creating it. Ralph might say this is not to create but to put outside what is already within. The bird has always existed in his mind; it is all to do with the floating helixes and the way in which memory is formed.

Mannie tried to grasp this particular theory, listening patiently as Ralph searched for the words and then when the words ran out she stared intently at the drawings, hoping that the meaning would leap out at her.

Ralph began to hear a crashing of waves, the roar of a tide as it broke on the island's rocky shore. He surmised that it might be the liquid in his brain – the sensation of cerebral fluid crashing against the contours of his skull. He was afraid that soon his thoughts (the essence of his identity) would be drowning, rather than swimming, in this liquid.

And, what of the rest of his body – the container of so much essential activity? What if the container withdrew, to be washed up on his island beach and left to rot, or – even more terrifying – to be picked at by the dark-winged bird? Would there be anything left of the essence of his identity?

Ralph held his head in his hands as he anguished over this. The thoughts tried to consolidate within the structure of words, but the structure began to elude him. He was in a fog of complex thought that resisted speech. The sense of what he wanted to say remained within him, almost as a physical sensation.

It was the frustration of not being able to verbally express his fears that made Ralph aggressive. How could he explain to Mannie about the crashing of waves and how the sound disturbed him? Ralph had never been one for the sea; he loved the countryside, the feel of grass beneath his feet, the solidity of land.

Nothing feels solid now. Not even the ward exists for Ralph and in his perception Mannie sits in the middle of his island terrain – except it isn't Mannie that he sees but a fuzzy, pink shape obscuring his limited vision. With this limited vision he needs to search for Amy – a familiar smudge of grey that can morph into a tiny bird, or a shadowy figure. On his more lucid days Ralph can grasp that Amy is a presence; a human presence.

Just now, having refused her walk, Amy has fallen asleep. She dozes with her head lolling to one side – her arms and legs slightly shuddering. Mannie grasps at this reprieve from constant interruption.

'Do you remember the bridge?' she asks, pointing once again to the postcard.

The question is an expression of her longing for her husband to remember something of their shared past. She has shed many bitter tears over this, feeling that her loss is almost greater than Ralph's. Their joint memory is severed down the middle and Mannie is left with the consciousness of what has been destroyed.

Ralph shakes his head. This is not a 'no', it is a confused response to the pink blur. He is trying to work out if the shape is a gentle, fluffy bird that twitters before him. He shivers as the creature ruffles its feathers and brushes softly against his skin.

'The bridge – at Courbevoie,' Mannie continues. 'It was such a beautiful summer's day. A bit like today but less humid. We walked by the river Seine and you talked about Seurat, about his fascination with the colour theories of ... what was his name?' Mannie stops for a moment, troubled by her own loss of memory.

'Chevreul! That was his name.' Mannie sighs. She does not remember much about Chevreul; only that Ralph went through a stage of reading his work. Chevreul had been a prolific writer on many subjects but it was his influence upon Seurat and other artists that had first captivated Ralph. Mannie had quietly thought to herself that it was enough for her to look at a painting without knowing the whole history of how it had come to be.

Mannie never voiced this opinion to Ralph. She is not one of life's innovators but she has been the constant in her husband's life. Ralph talked to Mannie about all sorts of ideas, some she grasped, some she couldn't, but she sensed it was important for him to articulate what was going on in his mind. She knew that her husband's mind was a strange mixture of intellect and intuition and that this was the brew that produced genius.

Where is Ralph's intellect now – torn to shreds by the remorseless pecking of the dark bird? And as for his intuition, it is pared down to the ability to grasp the difference between warmth and abrasiveness.

Baby Catherine

Chevreul resists detaining Madame Dupont for long. Just enough time for her to check him over, straighten his waistcoat and fluff out his cravat.

'Just think Monsieur Chevreul, the baby will be born on your hundredth birthday, now there's a coincidence!'

Madame Dupont doesn't quite understand the mind behind Chevreul's fame. She recognises that he is a learned man, bookish and given to 'deep' thoughts. Every time she lights a candle she remembers that it is thanks to Chevreul's discoveries, as a chemist, that the wax burns brighter and cleaner than it might have done. Whenever she picks up a bar of soap she knows that it comes cheaper because of Chevreul. Even the manufacture of fat for the pastries, that had to be made for the party, was originally due to Chevreul's inspiration. Little wonder he had been awarded the Légion D'Honneur and that his hundredth birthday is an occasion for national celebration.

'He is very deep,' she tells friends, with a shrug of her shoulders and upward flick of her pudgy hands. This gesture seems to imply that 'deep' could mean anything. Chevreul's mind is a twisting, labyrinthine space. Madame Dupont can only stand at the edge of it and wonder.

'I will see to it that the little one wants for nothing,' he assures her as she tightens the ribbons on her bonnet and makes for the door.

'You are too kind, Monsieur Chevreul. But the world knows it. Can you hear the sound of the crowds getting ready to celebrate?'

His hearing is not so good these days, but he can sense an excited buzz. And somehow, over the top of this, he thinks he can hear a baby's cry.

'You must make haste; your grandchild has arrived. Today is a double celebration indeed.'

Berthe had not understood about the game with the doll and had to be woken from a drunken sleep.

'The pain be natural,' Berthe declared, as she staggered about with pans of water.

'Give me some absinthe,' Marie screamed. 'Mama said I could have a drop of absinthe to ease the pain.'

'All right, all right! Now don't swig it mind – else you won't be able to push.'

Marie squinted at Berthe. 'Push – what do you bloody mean? Won't the baby just swim out?'

Berthe roared with laughter. 'Swim – what do you mean by swim? Babies don't swim into the world child! Didn't your mother explain anything to you?'

'The baby be in water,' Marie pouted, close to tears. 'I know the baby be in water.'

'The baby be in water no more!' Berthe announced. 'What do you think this puddle be in the bed?'

Marie didn't know what the puddle was; she thought perhaps she had wet herself.

'A dry birth is always the worst,' Berthe continued, 'take another drop – before things get harder.'

The baby didn't swim, it seemed to Marie that it tore and clawed its way out of her.

'A girl,' Berthe proclaimed, 'another poor wretch come into the world.'

Marie looked at the child. She stared hard at the little red face, the puckered mouth. Then Marie did something she rarely did – she smiled, and for a fleeting second the look of insolence was wiped from her face.

'She be prettier than my doll,' Marie declared, 'I shall call her Catherine. She be the nicest thing I have ever seen.'

Butterflies

Baby Catherine, Ralph's grandmother, was born into the poverty and squalor of Parisian life – but with the saving grace of Chevreul's protection. Chevreul was to live for another three years and during this time he developed a close bond with Marie Dupont's baby. The consequences of Chevreul's protection of the Dupont family are mapped within Ralph's floating helixes.

'The child is to have an education,' Chevreul declared one day.

Marie had accompanied her mother to Chevreul's rooms at the museum, allowing Catherine to play on the lawned gardens that could be seen from the window. What did this patch of green represent to the Duponts, accustomed to the dank and fetid atmosphere of city life?

'It is like nothing you've seen,' Madame Dupont informed Berthe.

Berthe nodded and declined to put the effort into summoning an image. A blank mental space seemed adequate to grasp at the unknown.

'I think this idea of learning be stupid!' Marie butted in. She loved her child, but her mind had not developed with her initiation into motherhood.

To Marie's simple view of the world Chevreul's money

represented lace edged dresses for the baby, adequate food and playthings that only the rich could afford – such as the gift of a beautifully crafted doll's house. Inwardly, Chevreul knew that the present would probably bring more pleasure to Marie than to her child. And it was so. Marie spent hours playing with the doll's house, extending her imagination to the notion of being a fine lady, who glided from one spacious room to another and had servants at her behest.

Baby Catherine plays on the lawn, while her grandmother, Elise Dupont, delivers soup and fresh rolls. Chevreul watches the child and he sees a mind unformed. It is his belief that there are divine sparks within each mind; that the sparks exist as surely as God exists and that they are waiting to explode into a pyrotechnic show of fire and light. He wants to ignite this potential, knowing from his own experience the value of a mind that has stretched itself to the limits.

The toddler already sees much of what Chevreul desires her to see. Her dark brown eyes, flashing like her mother's, but devoid of the insolent stare, focus on a butterfly resting on a flower. The child is mesmerised by the sense of shapes moving, merging. She waves her tiny arms up and down; her whole body shakes with excitement as she lets out a shriek of delight.

Chevreul thinks to himself that here is the essence of 'vision'. Here is the state that humans search for, and retreat to, in an effort to inhabit innocence once more. He shuts his eyes and dozes. He is a little weary for it is a hundred years since he was an infant like Catherine. It would be nice to stop thinking, to simply be, to experience pleasurable moments free from rational thought. He is also in great pain; his throat hurts, it gags when he tries to talk. He knows that there will not be many more words, written or spoken.

The butterflies flit in the garden outside of Ward B. If Chevreul's theory were wholly correct there should be a sense of repose amongst its inhabitants, but Ralph would say that 'going back' is not the same process as 'thinking back'; that the experiences we encounter during the formation of memory and making sense of our relationship to the external world, are of a different nature to the terrors we might encounter in the reverse process of severance from all that we know.

Ralph has entered a different state of knowing. He has a new mission in life – to control the tides on his island.

One of the hardest situations that Mannie endeavoured to deal with when caring for Ralph at home was his increasing fear of water. After a while she gave up on baths, as just the sight of her turning on the tap disturbed Ralph. Mannie wondered if she fussed too much, feeling that she should just let Ralph be, but she struggled to believe that this was what he really desired – to be left in pools of urine and smears of excrement.

Besides, Mannie could not cope with the smell. The smells no longer bothered Ralph; he recognised them as the smells of a prior, primitive existence.

Mannie's anxiety is also attached to the thought that had plagued Ralph the most when he was first diagnosed. What happened when he was unable to attend to his bodily functions? Ralph had always had a certain anxiety connected with going to the toilet because of a painful muscle sphincter complaint. The only time this problem receded was when he and Mannie went on walking holidays. The Northumberland moors were their favourite spot and for some reason Ralph seemed able to relax in nature. Squatted down, hidden by ferns and gorse bushes, he was able to relieve himself without pain.

Mannie had often joked about making a compost toilet in the garden, in fact − why bother with the niceties of formalising things, seeing as the garden was an acre of long grasses, wild flowers, weeds and brambles? As the illness progressed, Ralph instinctively took himself off to squat in the overgrowth. Mannie was inwardly a little dismayed, mainly because she didn't know how it was all going to end. It ended by Ralph not being able to remember where his squatting place was; he relieved himself when he needed to, and wherever − but often this caused him pain and he needed assistance.

Mannie's upset became akin to the squawking of seagulls. Ralph put his hands over his ears and screamed at her, a frustrated, incoherent scream. He had no words for his frustration but the sense of a thought painfully pinched his mind.

'What was wrong with this vociferous creature, didn't it understand that the tides swept everything away?'

Drowning

Tick ... tick ... tick ....

Only minutes have passed on Ward B since Mannie's arrival. It is an uneventful afternoon. Mannie arrives and is offered a cold drink. She pulls her chair around because Amy gets on her nerves and has already made a fuss, dropping her drinking beaker, but is now dozing. Mannie has not long taken the photo album out of her shopping bag before Ruth approaches her.

'Mannie,' she begins in a low whisper, glancing in Margaret's direction. 'I feel awkward asking, but we're short staffed and the nurse who was supposed to give Ralph his bath hasn't got round to it. I wondered if you might help me – just to try and keep him calm?'

Water laps around the edges of Blue-Grey Island. In his mind, Ralph spends most of his time regarding the liquid mass with hostility. He senses that you can drown in water; he is afraid the level of the water will rise and that the crashing of waves will engulf the rocks that protect him.

Ralph's imagination is not fettered by illness; it continues to create its own fantastical landscapes from the base substance of everyday reality. It roots around in his unconscious and draws out ghosts from the past. But of greater significance, the free-play of imagination liberates Ralph into an internal world, where he is still has the physical ability to walk and the gift of clear sight.

Sometimes, he moves to the centre of the island where he sits motionless. The consultant talks to Mannie about catatonic states as he leans over Ralph and shines a light in his eyes. Mannie knows that Ralph is not catatonic, that the state of rigor is a result of a conscious attempt not to move. She has watched him going into these states over the years and is sensitive to the fact that there is 'something' behind this strange, yet focussed behaviour, that she can't quite fathom.

Ruth brings a wheelchair to the bedside. Ralph feels his body being lifted. In his perception he has been grabbed from his hiding place by two birds; they hold him loosely in their beaks. It is not too uncomfortable because they are conjured as affable pelicans with soft fleshy gullets.

Now, Ralph feels that he has broken away from familiar surroundings. He wants to cry 'help' but the word eludes him. Panic has set in. Why, he inwardly protests, are the pelicans taking him away from his safe place on the island and do they not understand they are endangering him by moving him closer to the water?

A part of Ralph, which exists outside of our usual understanding of memory, senses that he is being taken somewhere threatening. How does this take place? Ralph has held on to his sensory memory; a patchwork of primitive, instinctive responses that remain locked in his body. These responses are severed from the mental recall of specific events.

Mannie remembers the consultant discussing this process at the beginning of the illness and how Ralph had taken the information in, understood what it meant, and even developed the idea further; suggesting that the imagination was able to function apart from the conscious mind. Ralph argued that the imagination and the unconscious mind worked in unison, eventually becoming omnipotent in a condition like dementia, taking over from reason and rationality.

At the hospital's request Ralph agreed to regular follow-ups with a psychiatrist who specialized in dementia. Mannie wasn't altogether comfortable with the arrangement. The consultant, a personable individual called Peter, had an immediate rapport with Ralph, but Mannie questioned whether this was because her husband's intellect still shone through.

How would they cope, Mannie wondered, the three of them in a room, when the inevitable deterioration set in? Despite the interpersonal warmth, she sensed the hard edge of science and academia. Something in Mannie resisted the notion of her husband becoming the subject of a research paper – even though she knew Ralph would probably enjoy nothing more.

Mannie had a dream that she could only intuit as territorial. In her dream, a door in Peter's office, a room that could almost be described as cosy, opened onto a dark corridor. Mannie walked the length of the corridor, a seemingly endless walk, until she reached another door leading into a laboratory. The laboratory had numerous shelves upon which jars were stacked. She instinctively knew, from within her dream state, that the jars contained brain specimens and tried to wake herself up – but not before she had been forced to look at the contents.

A queasy sensation persisted after the dream along with a growing resentment that her life with Ralph was going to be scrutinised. But she kept these thoughts to herself and agreed to keep a brief record of how her husband was doing between appointments.

At the end of 1987, almost a year into the illness, Mannie noted a change over the Christmas period. To an outsider it would not be so obvious because Ralph's ability with words meant he could, in a sense, 'cover up' some of his difficulties. But spatially he was having problems – simple tasks like getting dressed and setting the table were confusing him. Keeping their sense of humour, they had laughed together over the performance of organising a Christmas dinner for the family; as Mannie followed Ralph around re-organising place mats and crackers and retrieving bowls and dishes that didn't quite make it to the table.

That autumn Ralph had surprised everyone by being able to deliver a short address to the local Catholic Society for Cosmology Enthusiasts. Mannie had worried about the stress of attempting this but Ralph was determined, explaining that he had known many of the members for a long time and considered them as friends. He spent weeks preparing, lapsing into exhaustion and frequently asking for assistance with dates and pieces of information.

Mannie realised that Ralph was reminiscing whilst preparing his notes and wondered if the task had become a form of therapy. When he announced that he had finished the paper he seemed calmer – as though some worrying issue had been resolved within his mind. At the actual meeting Ralph was happy for a friend to read the address. Mannie decided that the challenge of putting the words together was more important to Ralph than the actual performance, and she wondered about the many thoughts that had gone into producing a few pages of writing; thoughts and feelings that had not been voiced or written down – or perhaps deleted because they were too hard hitting concerning his illness.

By the New Year, Ralph was more absorbed with his drawings and painting. The visual image was fast replacing words. Mannie wrote down in her record for Peter, 'January 1988, Ralph now likes to spend a lot of time on his own, painting. He gets a bit frustrated if I ask him about his work because it makes him sad and angry when he can't remember words. He used to love discussions but all of that is hard for him now. But at least my husband has an alternative form of expressing himself.'

Mannie paused for a moment and then scribbled out the last sentence. It felt like too much personal information.

During the spring of 1990, the deterioration in Ralph's ability to express complex thoughts accelerated, though there had been periods of stability. Mannie felt that she could no longer trust the prognosis of how long the process of deterioration would take, because the staging posts kept shifting. Secretly, she held onto the hope that Ralph might defy the odds by maintaining his sanity longer than predicted.

'We must take this with us,' Ralph declared, holding up a new painting.

The painting was of a chain-link structure. There were six links in the chain, loosely arranged. Ralph had repeatedly painted over the links in black, so that they stood out in sharp focus against a pale yellow background. Then he filled in the tiny oval gap, between the join in each link, with red crayon.

'Here,' he pointed to the tiny red ovals, 'here is my memory.'

Ralph needed reminding of Peter's name before each appointment. Mannie wasn't sure that Ralph actually remembered Peter at all from one encounter to the next, but the fabric of the relationship appeared to remain intact. Once in Peter's presence Ralph seemed to recognise that he was with someone who cared and was interested to understand his experiences.

In a much earlier consultation Ralph had challenged the assumption that language becomes inaccessible and incomprehensible with dementia, though he conceded that interpretation was difficult. He had agreed with Peter that it was essential for the listener to know something of the dementia patient's background and life events, and that as the patient slipped further and further into a surreal world even that 'inside' knowledge might not be enough to maintain a connection.

Mannie can recall Ralph sitting opposite Peter, clutching the painting. She had felt nauseous, with a churning anxiety in the pit of her stomach. How, she fretted, was Ralph going to explain the painting when words eluded him and he shook and almost cried with the frustration of not being able to express himself? She knew that the time had come for her to be the interpreter, that she had half an idea of what Ralph was trying to explain, but she was mute as he gesticulated over the unrolled painting.

Peter sat for a while puzzling and then to her surprise asked Mannie if she would mind removing the gold chain that she wore.

'A present,' she murmured, a little embarrassed, 'an anniversary present – quite a long time ago.'

Ralph nodded and started to rock a little. The rocking had become a signal that he was concentrating hard on trying to remember something.

Peter took the necklace and pulled it taut. Mannie hoped the chain wouldn't snap but smiled encouragingly.

'When you pull it tight there is no space between the links,' he spoke directly to Ralph. 'But if I lay the chain down loosely – like this – it slackens and a small oval gap appears. I think I understand what you mean.'

Mannie felt a little more enlightened. Right from the start Ralph had tried to explain that he was beginning to inhabit a world where the links connecting words, and giving meaning, did not entirely fall away. There was still a signifying chain of meaning, but a direct awareness of the association between words was fading and could never be retrieved. He had ribbed Peter at their first meeting that psychoanalysis was hardly of use because the loss of memory was not repression – it was an irretrievable loss.

The links in the chain still existed but it was the tiny oval, the seemingly empty gap in the centre of the overlap, which became suffused with meaning, and ruled with an insidious intent.

Ralph free-falls into the gaps. He has a sensation of slowly drifting in space, only to disappear into a black hole due to the intensity of a sudden gravitational pull. It is like discovering the secret of space travel and the ability to inhabit different time zones. The excitement and the dread of it cause him to stammer and splutter. The gaps are booby-trapped; they are explosions going off in his mind.

At other times, the slightest noise startles, making him violently plunge into one of the gaps and it is as though he is in a deep river with torrents of water pounding his head. The current pulls him under as a whole chunk of his life's history flows over him, drowning him with its somatic and emotional associations.

And so it is when Mannie gives a sharp word; Ralph is immediately the small child afraid of his father's anger, of his mother's inability to cope. This all takes place at the level of sensation; he cowers on the floor, weeping and covering his head for protection against the blows. And Mannie is crying, saying she can't cope, just like his mother – except Ralph can't separate Mannie and 'mother'. None of this can be said, can be spoken and explained. It is all taking place within the space connecting a word or action to memory.

'Yes – it's all in the gaps,' Ralph assures Peter, circling his hands around his head.

Back then, Ralph had realised, from that 'knowing place', that soon he would no longer be able to explain that his responses were not totally mad.

Ralph senses that the wheelchair is taking him closer to danger. He has been removed from his safe place, where he can calm the tides, to another part of the island.

Ruth and Mannie push Ralph into the bathroom. He cries out and flings his arms about.

'There, there Ralph, it's going to be all right. Nobody is going to hurt you.' Mannie tries to calm him. It is a half-hearted attempt; she knows that this particular problem is a lost cause.

Ralph sees the white rock pools; soon they will fill with water and here he is tortured and terrified. This is where the memory is subterranean, as deeper and deeper Ralph sinks beneath the swirling sea. The gaps slither and slide. Ah – this one is safe. It is the embryonic pool within the belly of Camille Dupont, Ralph's mother. There is a flash of momentary calm, when Ralph stops struggling, allows the warm soapy water to trickle over his head, down his back.

'There you are sweetheart, not so bad,' Ruth soothes.

The moment is fleeting; Ralph's mind is forced into another gap and with it the half-recognised memory of a hand brutally forcing his head under water.

'Drown you little bastard, that'll teach you! Just drown!' the voice floats in the ether. No one can hear it, not even Ralph. But he feels its intention, in every fibre of his body.

Birdsong

If Ralph were free to choose, he would stay in the gap that is the memory of floating in his mother's womb.

Within this gap he hears the sweetest of birdsong, a sound that cannot be compared with the trilling of birds bounded to the earth. To Ralph's ears the sound that he hears is celestial. This intonation has been with him in his loneliest moments, from childhood through to adulthood. And if he could recall this fact, in a direct kind of way, he would say that it is the memory of his mother singing; that this is the sound he was born into and the cadence that he longs for, to lull him into death.

Little Catherine Dupont, Ralph's grandmother, did not take kindly to her studies. In the struggle between nature and nurture she had inherited more of Marie's tendencies than Chevreul could buffer during his contact with the child. Fortunately, her tutor, Monsieur Berri, was a patient man, endeared to Chevreul's humanitarian ideals and determined to make something of his charge.

'You be wasting your bloody time,' Marie fixes Monsieur Berri with an insolent stare. 'The money be wasted! All the child do is run around and sing all day.'

'Is that so?'

'Drives me mad – all that la,la,la-ing. She be singing one of those rhymes you taught her!'

Catherine stands in the corner. Her little fists are clenched tight; her body rigid with as much anger as a four-year-old can summon. A foot is gingerly pushed out until it meets with the leg of a chair. The chair clatters against the hard surface of the floor.

'You be spoilt!' Marie screams.

Monsieur Berri visibly flinches. He is a mild mannered man and dreads his visits to the Dupont household. Things have deteriorated since Chevreul's death a year ago. Elise Dupont has reverted to type. She hangs around with Berthe, neglects the house and leaves Marie to cope with Catherine when she can barely look after herself.

'How about if I take the child for a while, see what I can do?' Monsieur Berri suggests.

'What she be worth?' Marie enquires.

Berri knows that this is the enquiry of an infant, trapped within a woman's body, who has simply grown tired of a doll and wants to swap it for another toy.

'I'm sure we can come to some arrangement,' he replies, aware of his obligation to Chevreul and thankful that he won't have to visit the Duponts again for some time. Explaining to his wife, well there lay another problem but hopefully she wouldn't mind. They already had six of their own, what difference could another body make?

Little Catherine was a natural rebel. Left to the state school system she would have had a haphazard attendance at the primary school. Berri knew that there was no chance of the child raising herself to the status of the 'boursier', should she ever reach secondary school. The 'boursier', the clever scholar from a poor background was revered in France. Chevreul realised that the will towards this advancement of self was lacking in the Dupont family. Berri conceded within himself that his private tutoring was Catherine's only hope.

What had Chevreul envisaged for Catherine; perhaps that she might be a teacher – possibly choosing to return to her own class of people in order to do some good?

Berri realised at once that Catherine was not like the rest of the children. It was not that his offspring were regimented but his wife had instilled a certain form of order into the daily routine in order to survive the mere fact of having six children. Catherine had been left to run wild, to follow her own will. She would slip down from her chair as the other children sat alert with easels and chalk. And always she gravitated towards the music room. Soon she was playing by ear, and singing the little songs and rhymes that Berri had taught her.

'It is obvious the child has a gift for music,' Madame Berri mused. She had greeted Catherine's arrival with mixed feelings. She was an attractive little girl to be sure, with her dark, flashing eyes and copper curls – glinting red in the sun. But what a will! Madame Berri was used to the tantrums of children and was not herself an authoritarian. However, her measured tone bore little influence with Catherine and it was decided that if the child wanted to sit at a piano all day, then that was what she would be allowed to do.

Catherine remained with the Berri family until she was fifteen, repaying their kindness by running away to sing on the stage of Parisian music cabaret.

Monsieur Berri had pursued her at first, pleading with her to return but Catherine refused, insisting that she had found her niche in life. Then one bleak night – so the story went – Madame Berri was woken by the excited cry of a servant. A baby girl, tightly swaddled in a shawl, had been left on the family's doorstep. There was no note, but it was clear from the baby's features and hair colouring who her mother was.

Ralph's knowledge of his family history is rooted in these few sparse details; that his mother was abandoned at birth, deposited on the doorstep of a family who went by the name of Berri. His mother was christened Camille and went by the name of Dupont. She attended the local primary and the higher elementary and decided she might like to train as a nurse. Monsieur Berri gave the suggestion serious thought. Camille was too young to enter the diploma course for nursing and would require funding. Berri was happy to financially support his charge with the remains of a family trust fund set up by Chevreul, but secretly hoped that in the intervening period of time she might change her mind. The threat of war in Europe felt imminent and he was anxious that Camille would be drawn into volunteering with the French Red Cross.

Camille did not change her mind and as Berri feared she decided to join the Red Cross volunteers in 1918 – a point in time when women were admitted to the front line to assist doctors at the wound dressing stations. In common with many Red Cross volunteers Camille never spoke openly about her experiences. The horrors of trench war became a pact of silence between Ralph's parents. Thomas never spoke of Camille's bravery and calm capability, and Camille never spoke of the terror and vulnerability of the young soldier she fell in love with.

Only the birdsong survives from this story. It is the birdsong that has found its way into the double stranded helixes.

The Familiar

M annie would take comfort from knowing that it is the birdsong that Ralph hears in his calmer moments, even if this provides only a few seconds respite.

The consultant had stressed to Mannie that she must strive to 'keep up the familiar'. Mannie understood the essence of this but couldn't quite convey that the 'familiar' was a rather chaotic, topsy-turvy sort of existence. She sometimes felt that this was the result of their moving into the farmhouse at the beginning of the sixties. The only reason they had been able to afford the house was because Ralph was ten years her senior. He was in his early thirties and well established as a researcher and lecturer.

Mannie remembers their first encounter. She pictures herself, sitting at the desk in the reception department of the Science block at the University – typing. She sees Ralph, as he was then, a nervous man with an ample mop of untidy black hair and thick-rimmed glasses. It was the smile that drew her to him, a warm engaging smile. She had been smitten for weeks before he plucked up the courage to ask her out.

A speedy courtship followed; just six months from start to finish. What a whirlwind that had been. Mannie recalls Ralph turning up in his Ford Popular to collect her from home and the emotional excitement of a first date. She had been ready for hours and her father had teased that she would wear out the mirror in the hallway, as pink lipstick was replaced by peach, then orange, and back to pink again.

The car was Ralph's only claim to material possessions and Mannie sensed his pride as they drove through the Northumbria landscape, stopping off at a little teahouse on the way. She was to discover that Ralph loved to be close to nature and preferred exploring the countryside to any other leisure activity.

Sophia had teased about the age gap between her parents – an age gap that Mannie now feels has had an affect on her life. Not so much in her later years, she reasons, but in her youth when she might have gone down another road; a road signposted 'rock and roll', the road Sophia thinks she should have gone down.

'I was so shy,' Mannie explained to Sophia.

'But Mum – think of the sixties ambiance, the urge towards liberation and change – not to mention the cool fashion. Didn't you soak up any of that? Just think – you missed out on being a hippy, rock chick!'

'I was actually quite old by then Sophia.'

'Old – how old?'

'Well into my twenties, and things were very different a decade before, in the fifties, when I was a teenager.'

Mannie tried to explain some more. She had not spent long in the company of her female contemporaries, mainly composed of friends made at secretarial college. Even then the conversation had been dominated by an exchange of make-up tips over a cappuccino coffee. Mannie smiles at the recollection of what a grown up activity this had felt to be. There had been a certain panache to sprinkling the white froth with brown sugar whilst heatedly discussing which record to put on the jukebox. It was all for the sake of the local lads, this girlish brashness.

It took courage to walk over to the jukebox, nonchalantly. Mannie lacked the confidence and hung back. She agonised over her new slacks and jumper. Were the slacks too tight, the close-ribbed jumper a bit revealing? She recalls how she always felt slightly out of place and was instantly at home with Ralph's somewhat dreamy distance from contemporary youth culture. It was a great relief to be freed from having to choose an image.

Looking back on it now she wonders if Ralph was actually ahead of his time. Wasn't his attitude what the feminists most desired in a man? Her husband had never made her feel that she had to be anything other than herself. Mannie feels slightly abashed at having these thoughts; she wonders if they don't smack of complacency and concludes this is the reason why Sophia always seems irritated with her. Perhaps, her daughter thought her lazy – that she had never bothered to find her 'true' self?

Ralph had wanted the farmhouse. They had been married for a couple of years and had long outgrown his bachelor flat and now a new research post beckoned. Looking back, Mannie could see that the move had allowed them to become disorganised. Luxuriating in so much extra space they had spread their belongings through umpteen rooms without any sense of order. They had always intended to re-organise but it never happened.

'It is perfect,' Ralph had enthused and Mannie knew that this was true for him. From out of the attic window, they could see the church spire, an important symbol for her husband, and beyond that a southerly view of the heavens. On clear evenings Ralph sat close to the window's edge with his ten-inch Newtonian reflecting telescope, tracking the stars. Ralph explained to Mannie the principles behind the reflecting telescope; it was all to do with getting away from unwanted colour. Achromatic – that was the word, pure light. Equipping the observatory didn't come cheap as one telescope replaced another. Mannie couldn't quite get into the technicalities of the quality of eyepieces and other accessories.

After a couple of years the decision was made to construct a viewing platform. On moonlit nights Mannie sat out in the garden, enjoying the peace and waiting for the rustle of hedgehogs in the grass. She loved the wildlife that the garden attracted and felt little need for human companionship. High above her Ralph searched the night sky, on one occasion making her jump as he whooped with pleasure.

'Come see,' he shouted, 'the rings of Saturn!'

It was true – they were beautiful. And yet a sadness seemed to set in after this event.

'I cannot paint them,' Ralph declared. 'There are no colours to express what I have seen.'

The house remained tumbledown, the garden overgrown and at some level Mannie had to admit that this was also due to her. She had begun to enjoy the freedom of their rambling existence. Whilst others toiled, Ralph and she jogged along. It was relaxing, being with a man who simply appreciated having her around – who wanted to sit with her and share his thoughts. The sharing wasn't exactly equal but Mannie accepted that was part of the deal. The only pressure on Mannie was to be a good listener and she didn't mind this.

The consultant had said to keep up the familiar. Mannie began to discover that the familiar wasn't some generalised notion; that for Ralph and her it signified a complex web of interchanges and mutually accepted ways of living. The more deranged Ralph became the more unsafe Mannie felt within herself. Didn't the experts realise that the familiar was the relationship she and her husband had created together and that this was dying and that nothing would ever feel the same again?

Crows

In the weeks before his fall, if Ralph had realised that Mannie's insistence on sitting him down by the French doors, every morning after breakfast, was an attempt to introduce a regular routine that he might recognise as 'familiar', he would have asked her to refrain. Yes – there was a certain kind of familiarity, but not the sort that Mannie had intended.

It was whilst sitting by the French doors that Ralph began to have some of the strange and frightening experiences he had to endure on Blue-Grey Island. Mannie had not understood that positioning him by the glass doors made him vulnerable, because the birds could see him.

He caught sight of a bird, probably a messenger bird, flying towards him. It emerged from one of the white, fluffy clouds that floated suspended in the sky. Ralph was convinced that the clouds were the snow tipped mountains that dipped down to the sea surrounding his island.

Ralph no longer needed his telescope as nothing remained in the distance anymore. The bird flew out of the cloud and its tiny eyes, dark – like two jade gemstones – locked with his. Ralph felt his entire body sucked into the bird's line of vision, followed by a lifting sensation as he was carried away.

'Ah!' he called out in fear, attempting to rise from the chair.

Mannie came rushing in.

'Hush now, there's no need to be upset. Let's settle down and have a cup of tea together.'

Mannie looks at the clock. It is 10.30 a.m. She is weary, the morning is only half over and somehow she has to fill in the time with Ralph. As she leaves the room to fetch the tea, the clock strikes on the half-hour. Ralph shudders, he is beginning to sweat. He recognises the chime, what it signifies.

Every morning, at this time, the crows come. There is a tall tree on the island around which the crows circle, fighting amongst themselves as to which branch to settle upon. A magpie eyes the gang as it spreads its wings in readiness for attack. The creature opens its beak and the sound it emits resonates at the same pitch as machine gun fire. Ralph's ears fill with a rushing of air as the crows evacuate the tree, circle round and land again. On and on the battle continues, the sound of gunfire and the rushing of air. Ralph's attention is split between vision and sound as he oscillates between the roles of aggressor and victim.

This is a moment of paralysis, a gap that he plunges into, when he doesn't know whether to cower or fight. He is marching with a long line of people; he could be a master or he could be a slave, an SS officer or a holocaust victim. Ralph doesn't formulate his feelings with these words but the sensation that he experiences is attached to the paranoia of generations, and there is no paranoia without real persecution.

Ralph had been told many times the story of his father's capture and subsequent internment in France. He can no longer recall the factual details of the story but there are remnants laid down, fragments he grasps with his seemingly dissociated mind. The magpie's ominous rattle increases. Ralph clumsily raises his body from the chair, then stumbles.

'F... father!' he stutters, letting out a low moan.

Mannie rushes in and grasps Ralph's arm to steady him.

All she can see is the garden, silent and still now, but she knows that the crows disturb Ralph.

'It's all right my dear – they've gone now. Come and sit down.'

This was their morning vignette, before Ralph was admitted to hospital, before it reached the point where Mannie could no longer calm her husband.

If Ralph had been able to answer Mannie he would have explained that the birds had gone for one reason only; that the charred and blackened landscape of no-man's-land is not attractive to wildlife and hence the puzzle for him is how come this piece of terrain is part of his island?

Precious Things

Ralph shrieks and lashes out as he is hauled from the rock pools.

'Nearly finished,' Ruth states, more formal than usual. She has great patience but even her capacity for good humour is stretched to the limit on this sultry afternoon. Home beckons, the delights of her garden, and the temporary relief of being removed from the smells, sights and sounds of all this human distress.

'Well done Mannie. Just his pyjamas to pop back on, then we'll all have a well earned cup of tea.'

Mannie is inwardly distraught. The pink dress is literally sticking to her overheated body. Ralph has lost so much weight and she is afraid to let her eyes linger on his skeletal frame – the blue veins mapped across his parchment skin like some vast road system.

Ralph's suffering is inscribed upon his body. It is as though his flesh is melting away to reveal his inner disturbance. Part of Mannie wants all the suffering to be over. What would Ralph say to her now if he could express himself coherently? She struggles to believe that given the choice he would want to carry on.

'Remember the precious things,' he had said to her. 'Remember for both of us.'

Mannie has tried, but the immediacy of the present is wiping away all the happy memories. One of the ways she has attempted to keep her promise to Ralph is by recording her recollections. She had been a little self conscious about this process at the beginning, not being easily given to sentiment, and never having felt compelled to write her thoughts down in the past.

In this respect Ralph and she had been polar opposites. For Ralph, thoughts were like the snowflakes he had longed to capture as a child. Every thought was different, unique, and had the potential to form myriad pathways to further thought. There was no knowing where a thought might take you, so you had to capture it before it melted away. Mannie was used to Ralph's scribbles; on the backs of envelopes, the insides of cereal packets – anything that he could write upon.

This kind of spontaneity eluded Mannie and she had wondered where to begin. After Ralph's admission to hospital she cleared a small corner for herself at his desk in the attic; setting a space for a notebook bought from the village store. Mannie had scrutinized the cover on the notebook – a painting of a bunch of pansies placed in an ornate vase – and thought to herself that it was just the sort of painting Ralph would dislike.

She had opened the book and stared at the first blank page, hoping for inspiration. At intervals, she stood up from the desk and walked over to the casement window. It was January and the fields were frosted up. Ralph had once attempted to paint this 'whiteness'. Using Seurat's method he applied tiny dots of paint to the canvas but never seemed wholly satisfied with the result.

'White is not white,' he informed Mannie and she knew

that here was another thought to be pondered upon.

Mannie sat down once again; her mind jolted by the memory, and wrote the word *white* in the centre of the page. She found she was able to write more freely than she had anticipated.

White, my wedding dress was white. I debated within myself, was it wrong to wear white seeing as I wasn't a virgin anymore? And you laughed gently and stroked my face Ralph and said that in some way I would always be a virgin for you and that we would always have new territory to explore together.

That was a lovely time, waking together in our room in the cottage, next to the moor. And we had pretended to be man and wife, sharing our sweet, guilty secret, because it was still frowned upon then to have sex before marriage. Not that we had planned to make love. We had naively thought that we would just cuddle and sleep. We were both innocent and inexperienced, me because of my age – you because of your shyness and perhaps a few catholic scruples. I lay in your arms and felt sheltered, protected. Neither of us had anticipated the power of the attraction and sense of connection.

Mannie stopped writing and took a sharp intake of breath. The emotions lay heavy within her.

White: you said my skin was white. You ran your fingers down my back, across my thighs. It took a while for me to relax, to realise that it was permissible to have all those pleasurable sensations, but I was afraid to cry out in case the owner heard us. We were late down to breakfast and I felt that everyone else could see, could look straight through me to the part that had been pleasured by you. We ate our breakfast and talked in whispers. Later, walking on the moors you were happy, ecstatic. It seemed strange to me – that I could make another human being so happy. I felt so ordinary, unsure as to why you had chosen me, this bright individual who could have had his intellectual equal. But that was before I really understood you Ralph, experienced your pain and held you like a little child sobbing in my arms.

November 1987

Notes for annual address to the Catholic Society for Cosmology enthusiasts

1: Introduction – talk a little about my background

Over the past fifty years the seminal events in the history of astronomy and astrophysics, and man's endeavours to travel in space, have often occurred in tandem with important events in my personal life.

The year of my marriage, 1957, was the year of the launch of Sputnik 1 & 2. The launch of Apollo 11 in 1969, and the momentous event of man's first steps on the moon, coincided with the year of my daughter's birth. In between, Cold War politics softened into a tenuous détente as I struggled, within myself, to ease the relationship between religious cosmology and physical cosmology.

In 1986 Challenger exploded, in full view of the world, whilst at the same time (unbeknownst to me) a miniscule, yet lethal explosion, took place in my brain – the beginnings of vascular dementia, soon to be followed by the shattering news that I have early onset Alzheimer's.

Is it permissible to say this? Well these people are my friends

– for how long have I been giving talks to the Society? It feels like years and years. All the familiar faces will be there and we are a close community. The news will have filtered through. Have you heard, Ralph Drew – poor man – has early onset dementia? How will he cope – should he be giving a talk – will he embarrass himself?

I am still a mind that thinks, remembers – I have not yet fully lost my way.

2: Mention Hubble telescope

I wonder, will I be able to add the launch of the Hubble Telescope to my list of coincidences – due, as it is, to be launched in the foreseeable future – and with what event in my life might it coincide?

We astronomers have faith that Hubble will provide, at least in part, the answer to the composition of dark matter. This question has fascinated and perplexed me for much of my adult life. Will I be privileged to see with clarity that which I have searched for these past forty years, or will my own clarity of vision dim into obscurity just at the point at which Hubble provides us with deep field optics?

When Sophia was a child she loved dot-to-dot puzzles. She was a sharp little thing and soon learnt to identify the pictures in advance of joining up the dots.

'Look Daddy – it's a cat!' she announced, as the pencil moved swiftly from dot 1, to 2, to 3, etc.

Am I doing the dot-to-dot of my life in writing this and can I see the complete picture in advance?

I was born in 1927 against a backdrop of exciting discoveries. In 1915/16 Einstein published his General Theory of Relativity soon to be followed by Eddington's announcement that the observation of stars near the eclipsed sun confirmed general relativity's prediction, that massive objects bend light.

I drew a little stick man, an object and a star for Mannie, to illustrate this.

3: Talk a bit more about Einstein

In the 1920's, Friedman and Lemaitre independently formulated solutions to Einstein's field equations, which predicted an expanding universe. This was not just a scientific coup; philosophically it meant that the Universe – which had been viewed as fixed and immutable and therefore existing timelessly – actually had a history; most significantly a singularity – a beginning. The concept of time was now a central issue for science.

Time's arrow – I try to paint it. I am impaled on its tip. I am speeding into the void – free falling outside of the realm of physics. Does this mean I can travel faster than the speed of light? Do I inhabit more than one universe? I am confused.

In 1929, following Edwin Hubble's discovery of the isotropic expansion of the universe, Einstein was forced to acknowledge that the cosmos is not static. He struggled all his life to accept that the universe does not always conform to a deterministic law (especially in the realm of quantum mechanics) though his wonder at the creation led him to believe in 'the presence of a superior reasoning power' that ordered regularity in the natural world. But for Einstein this 'power' was not the God of the Bible.

I was just two years of age at the time of Hubble's discovery – hardly aware of what a thorny issue the potential divide between Religion and Science would become for me.

The concept of 'the Big Bang' and the expansion of the universe certainly fuelled the debate and this debate continues to our present time.

'Ok Pops – in one simple paragraph – explain the expansion of the universe.'

This was Sophia talking – hands on hips. Some school assignment I seem to remember. She didn't like to ask for my help – didn't want the other kids to think she was at an advantage.

Eyes sparkling and red hair flaming – my darling daughter.

4: Briefly explain the principles of gravity and expansion

Simply speaking, expansion causes cooling and atoms form from the molecules. Gravity draws the matter into larger and larger clumps. Now gravity may well pull things together, therefore slowing down expansion, but we now know some other force – elusive dark energy – is pushing things apart and this increases expansion.

The universe is not static but ideally requires a harmonious balance to survive. Too much expansion and it will overly cool, a state commonly referred to as 'the big chill'. Too little expansion and the universe will overheat – contracting to the point of implosion, an event referred to as 'the big crunch'.

Sophia and I played with a balloon, on which I had drawn small dots in order to demonstrate the principles of expansion and contraction. I wasn't sure that she'd understood my explanation but she enjoyed bursting the balloon! She was about eleven at the time. I remember Tony – my dear friend from college days – came to visit the next day, with his two boys Martin and David.

'Hey Dad – come and watch this!' Sophia commanded.

She was quite an organiser and a much stronger personality than the boys. Three chairs were lined up on the grass. Tony, Mannie and myself were told to sit down and be the audience.

The boys stood giggling but Sophia pushed Martin forward. 'Say your words!' *she bossed.*

'It is the birth of the world,' *Martin spoke hesitantly.*

Sophia looked annoyed. 'Universe not world,' *she mouthed in Martin's direction, and then,* 'now you David.'

David was a sweet child, a couple of years younger. I remember he shouted, rather than spoke his words.

' *The universe was just a tiny little dot and then there was a big ex ... explosion and after a long time lots of planets and stars were born from all the bits of matter.'*

The children charged off – running around, making explosive sounds.

Sophia took centre stage and clearly spoke what must have been some well-rehearsed words. 'After the explosion everything started to cool down and without gravity all the *bits of matter would have drifted further and further apart – and the universe would have got really cold.'*

Then the children skipped in different directions to the edges of the lawn.

'This is called the big chill,' Martin chimed, before they all raced to the centre of the lawn and bumped into each other jostling for space.

'And this is called the big crunch!' Sophia beamed, 'the opposite of really cold.'

Next, they all held hands as though they were about to play a Ring a Ring 'o Roses, but they actually walked quite sedately in a circle.

'What's this one Pops?' Sophia asked me. She always called me Pops when she was being a bit cheeky – in an affectionate way.

'Now let me see,' I replied, 'would it be harmonious balance?'

David glanced at Sophia confused; I think he had grown tired of the game or possibly hadn't understood it. After all, charging around pretending to be a clump of matter isn't normally of interest to a nine year old.

'There are some special words – you told me some special words dad.' Sophia persisted.

I could see that Mannie was looking strained and irritated. She was probably wishing that Sophia didn't need to try and impress me this way.

'Well – do you mean critical density?' I ventured with more enthusiasm than I truly felt.

The boys were definitely bored by now – having dropped holding hands and generally scuffing the grass with their trainers.

There was no doubt that Sophia could be precocious.

'Uncle Tony – you know it, one word begins with O and is in a different language.'

'Ah – you mean Omega equals one?' Tony suggested, 'the optimal state for the survival of the universe.'

He gave me a look as though to say, 'this one is going to be following in your footsteps.' But he was wrong about that.

5: The debate triggered by the discovery of the expanding universe

The debate on the future of the universe post big bang felt revolutionary to me in my twenties, when I was starting out as a scientist. We had been so accustomed to the laws of Newtonian physics, some would say reflecting biblical laws, set down in perpetuity. But the evidence for expansion became incontestable.

The Catholic Church, indeed any religious sector of society, had to take the above on board and think through the implications of such a theory for faith and belief. If the universe had a beginning then it wasn't necessarily eternal – so what happened to the notion of a 'world without end'? Also, for some, Einstein's denial of the existence of a personal God or indeed any supernatural force that had willed 'the big bang' was unnerving.

Einstein's goal was to unify the laws of nature under a single model, which was to be drawn from empiricism. Today – physicists search for 'a theory of everything' and metaphysics struggles to have a voice.

Einstein – I can still see him in my mind's eye. My long-term memory holds good even if I did start my day by putting

washing in the fridge. It hardly seems possible – that these small aberrations are indicative of so much worse to come. My balance is off centre – there is a slight numbness in my left foot – I seem to shuffle rather than walk.

I wonder what's happening in my brain – the big crunch or the big chill?
… And is the will of God the same as Omega equals one?

6: The central issue concerning science and faith

From my twenties onwards I began to tackle the issue that concerned me most, namely my belief that 'the mind of God' cannot be known through factual knowledge; and that it is not helpful to try and prove/disprove God's existence through logical deduction or the principles of physics.

I would venture that God is truly experienced through 'relationship' and that our vehicle for this is the grace of prayer.

There was no point in trying to explain this to Einstein, who argued that prayer was just a way of talking to the educated part of the self – the altruistic part attached to core values and a sense of the common good.

This doesn't help me now – not when I'm walking through the 'valley of the shadow of death.'

How does this 'relationship' fit with another core belief I hold, based on the conviction that scientific fact has to be 'free' in relation to the source of faith – in this case the Bible.

Are there any parallels between prayer and empiricism or are they opposed activities?

I believe the Bible has to be understood as symbolic, a moral discourse, and therefore it is not a deterministic text.

When we bit into 'the tree of knowledge', gaining access to an understanding of good and evil, we bit into uncertainty and working with uncertainty is fundamental to faith. But I would suggest there is also an element of uncertainty built into scientific endeavour.

Freedom of interpretation, within any sphere, means living with uncertainty and perhaps it is the creator's will, even down to Quantum physics, that we learn to live with a quota of inconclusiveness. The fully determined is not necessarily the most beautiful, perfect or wise.

7: Share when my uncertainty began and my visit to Princeton in 1946

As a young man, I travelled to Princeton to hear Einstein speak. I was fortunate enough to be awarded a term at an American College, as an exchange student. At that time I was struggling to hold onto my belief in a personal God. I could see how it might be construed as illogical to posit a caring God post Holocaust, Nagasaki, and Hiroshima. Even setting aside scientific discourse – a discourse that for some collapses faith – there seemed to be so much evil and discord in the world. On a more personal level I'd seen tragedy strike a dear friend.

I kept asking myself, did a God who was meant to be omnipotent, and therefore able to intervene at the level of miracles in the natural order and in the life of the individual, have to necessarily be interventionist?

This question troubles me now. It seems that God's intervention is rarely of an obvious nature. Even Christ on the cross felt forsaken.

My conviction had been easily sustained as a child. My mother was a committed Catholic and I was brought up in that heavily ritualistic atmosphere that is the Catholic Church.

For my mother and I the church building provided a place of warmth and peace, and the relationships we formed with other members provided an extended family. I took comfort from this because there were difficulties at home; my father could be aggressive and on occasions violent.

Dad – he never came to my confirmation. He skulked about in the hallway as Mum neatened my hair and brushed down the shoulders of my new jacket. That had caused a rumpus – the new jacket. Mum had been saving for it for months. She wore the usual – a navy polka dot dress and a matching pill box hat. She pulled the net down over her eyes, but I could see that she had been crying – and that soft mouth was twitching.

I see my childhood as a state of innocence concerning my belief in a personal God. It did not appear illusory or fantastical at the time that by closing my eyes, and commencing a ritual called prayer, I could conjure up a living presence within my mind with whom I could communicate.

I try not to underestimate the power of this child-like state, for it is what we may return to when the external intellectual debate and the internal rumination, that brought us to this belief or that point of view, is lost to our recall. The rational mind imposes many layers of thought – as does the external world – but they may all fall away as death approaches.

Death. Einstein did not appear afraid of death. In fact, he held that we must let go of our hope and our fear to be truly open to what he termed 'cosmic religiosity'.

In my first year, as an undergraduate, I read Einstein's view on religion and on paper he argued well. He described himself as an Agnostic – or 'deeply religious non-believer'. In his words he had a 'deeply emotional conviction of the presence of a superior reasoning power'.

The man unsettled me

I could not disagree with Einstein, that there is a problem when religious doctrine makes dogmatically fixed statements on subjects that belong in the domain of Science.

'Arguing against dogma, that's the easy bit,' I recall saying to Tony, as we travelled by train.

It feels like yesterday, the journey Tony and I made to Princeton. We were debating to pass the time.

'But don't you feel that Einstein borrows from religion, particularly Christianity, in order to express his ideas?' I continued.

Tony swayed side to side with the motion of the train.

'You mean when he writes about the cosmic religious feeling that fires art and science but that isn't connected in any way to an anthropomorphic view of God?'

'Yes,' I replied, swaying in unison. 'He does this strange inversion. In his view the geniuses who are in touch with this cosmic feeling have freed themselves of a dogma of a God that is any way connected to humankind.'

'Go on,' Tony encouraged.

We probably looked a bit comical to the other passengers, an elderly gentleman and a young couple with a sleeping baby.

'Well,' I continued, 'my understanding of the Bible is that man is created in God's image, but that we struggle to mirror the essence of God through an appraisal of human qualities because humans are always lacking. Surely to be a mirror for God's qualities is a lifetime's quest?'

Tony sat silent for a while – he never rushed for words – so I hurried on.

'To be made in God's image, spiritually and morally, does not guarantee that we stay within the mould. Free will and therefore the freedom to choose between good and evil can shatter the mould to pieces.'

'Yes, that may be so Ralph,' Tony proffered, 'but Einstein argues that there is no necessary relation between religion and ethical behaviour and some might argue that even the supreme force does not always choose good; so what happened to God's essential nature? Is the mirror itself an illusion?'

'I understand that,' I remonstrated, 'but even Einstein seeks out a transcendental 'mirror'. He writes that we have to have 'the living spirit' within us in order to act within traditional values.'

The elderly gentleman shuffled in his seat, sighed and opened his newspaper. Not to be put off, Tony leaned forward indicating that I should reply in a whisper.

'I think Einstein wants it both ways,' I continued less effusively, 'an element that is supra-personal, but not connected in anyway with a divine being, yet an element that by definition does not require, and is not capable of, rational explanation.'

'So – you would argue that Einstein has failed to fully work out the co-relationship between science and religion, despite the fact he acknowledges they are related yet separate spheres?'

I nodded in agreement.

'And,' Tony continued, ' though he acknowledges that the two magisteria of religion and science overlap – it is not in a way that supports a faith in a personal God. This is no doubt too simplistic a view for you Ralph – but less problematic for an atheist like me.'

I miss Tony.

8: Talk about Einstein and free will

Grappling with Einstein helped me to re-define my religious faith. The greatest flaw in his argument (I feel) is that he never fully pursues the notion of free will – either God's ability to intervene in a presumably fixed order of nature, at the level of miracle, or man's ability to negate moral law.

Einstein wanted a world in which we are all capable of acting from a position of the 'living spirit' within us – but I cannot see any other way of accessing this 'living spirit' other than by God's presence in my life, in my inner world. Revelation is surely more than tradition. Revelation takes place within dialogue and dialogue is crucial to prayer.

'Yeh, yeh Pops – whatever you say.' Sophia teasing me – she was about sixteen. Red hair dyed black. Charcoaled eyes – a dark line drawn across her lids. 'Revolution – now that's the road to revelation.'

What is revealed to us through prayer is the revelation of a personal God whose spiritual presence and guidance takes us beyond our limited human state and can encourage us to re-work tradition.

But we are always free – to choose to embrace or ignore this relationship as a guiding power in our lives.

Sophia chose to ignore. In many ways she was more questioning than I had been as a child. I think she rattled the nuns with her objections during confirmation classes and it wasn't long after that when she firmly told me that the Catholic faith wasn't for her.

I didn't mind too much that she rejected Catholicism – but a belief in any faith would have done. I don't like to think of her out in the world without some comfort and protection.

When I think about it now I wonder if I clung too much to the culture I was brought up in. Perhaps Catholicism is just the familiar peg I hang my faith upon? I can see clearly now that its just one of many routes to an awareness of spirit. Just one of 'many stories', as Tony would have put it.

9: Summing up after floor discussion

All true discovery involves a leap of faith – the maths tends to follow. In our spiritual lives we lack the maths, the tangible proof of God's existence, but this is where we trust the experience of our inner life – that subterranean world that can never be wholly visible to the human eye.

Einstein's ghost still unsettles me.

I do not know whether to pray for a miracle.

Reminiscence Therapy

Some parts of the island are scarier than others. Ralph's distress diminishes once he is back on the ward because it is a less anxiety-provoking space. Amy, despite being a greyish blur that can take on several forms in Ralph's perception, is a comforting presence.

Mannie glances at the clock. She is an hour into her visit. Amy, now awake from her nap, has resumed babbling with increased vigour. Mannie decides to try again with the Reminiscence album. The album is a condensed version of all the other albums back home, a well-intentioned attempt to remind Ralph of the particulars of his family narrative. There had been a point to the exercise earlier in the illness, but once more Mannie pushes aside the thought that the album is not of much use now.

There is a photo of Ralph's father on the first page. He has been photographed standing, with a group of fellow miners, by the winding gear at the pit's surface. Mannie is unsure about the photo, wonders if she should have included it, but has come to the conclusion that not to do so is a denial. Alongside it, on the opposite page, is a studio portrait of Ralph's mother. Mannie couldn't fathom what had drawn this pretty, diminutive young woman to Thomas Drew.

'See Ralph, your mother and father,' she points to the photo. 'Can you pick your father out from his work mates?'

Ralph stares – perplexed.

'They all look the same,' Mannie continues, 'with their weathered faces and peaked caps.'

On the back of the photo Ralph's father had scribbled in his uncertain hand – *Tommy and mates outside Dovecot Colliery – 1916.*

'But Tommy does stand out; he's more stocky than the others.' Mannie takes Ralph's hand and places it on the photo. 'And your mother, doesn't she look lovely? That's who you got your gentle eyes from Ralph.'

Mannie wonders what Camille must have made of England, of Northumberland. The beauty of the place might have won her over, but the barrier of language – how had she coped with that? Even a fine command of the English language could not help with getting to grips with the northern dialect. Yet Camille had coped. Mannie could clearly recollect her mother-in-law's voice, the soft Geordie lilt that was merely enhanced by the trace of a foreign accent.

She remembers their first meeting; how she was slightly taken aback by Ralph's background, as it was much poorer than her own. Camille had made the best of her tiny home, consisting of four rooms in all with no bathroom or inside toilet. There were odd touches of finery, betraying a longing for something more – not that this was ever selfishly expressed. Mannie thinks of the first time she took Ralph's mother shopping in Newcastle. They had headed straight for Fenwick's, one of the big department stores, and Camille had stood transfixed like a child in a

Christmas grotto until she eventually chose some chair back covers. Mannie remembers they were delicately stitched with a daisy design.

'To save me the trouble of embroidering!' Camille had laughed, linking Mannie's arm in her own.

When they returned home Camille laid out the covers to show Ralph's father.

'Such lovely colours Thomas, far better than anything I could sew.'

Thomas raised half a smile as he sat hunched in the corner of the room near to the television screen. The television had been a present from Ralph in the hope that it might curb his father's drinking habits; keep him more at home than in the pub.

'Such lovely colours,' Camille quietly repeated as she put the covers away.

Black was the predominant colour in Thomas Drew's mind. Perhaps this was not always so, in his infant years, when he had run free with the other children in the village. He was the fifth child of George and Minnie, the fifth to be placed in a wooden drawer next to his parents' bed in the terraced house provided by the colliery. Too soon the time came to join his father and siblings down the pit; a dark world of heat, sweat and grime.

As a child, Ralph had tried to imagine this alien world. Once, when his father was sleeping, he crept up to the bedside. Thomas was breathing heavily, the smell of liquor wafting into the surrounding air. Ralph held his imaginary telescope up to his eye and focused hard on his father's forehead. Here was a strange terrain, an undulating landscape of weathered skin. Here lay the memories of

Thomas Drew's attempted escape from colliery life, years before his son was born.

Ralph had known how the story went. The Miners' Union finally agreed to the enlistment of colliery workers, towards the end of the First World War, and Thomas was amongst the first to volunteer. Ralph wondered what his father had felt as he pulled on his khaki uniform? He thought possibly a sense of exhilaration at escaping life at home. It did not seem likely to Ralph that his father would have had any sense of fear.

The feelings of Thomas's mother were missing from the brief narrative. Ralph's grandmother had presented his father with a waistcoat and gloves, which she had hurriedly knitted. This act had felt like stepping back in time for her, seizing the opportunity to be motherly, concerned and proud, rather than wretched and downtrodden. All of the men folk in her family drank to excess and Thomas was no exception. The new laws governing drinking hours, heralding drunkenness as an enemy of war production, had done little to improve life at home. Sometimes her son was affectionate when drunk, but mostly he displayed a wicked temper.

Mannie has not included a photo of Ralph's grandparents in the album. She figures that one generation of family misery is enough to try and remember.

Dangerous Places

Ralph found, as his illness progressed, that he was filling in pieces of knowledge about his father that he had not been able to fathom as a child. His first glimpse of the MRI scan elicited fear and a recognition that here lay a dangerous place. An absence of danger had been what his father most begrudged about Ralph's existence. 'That – and my having been born at all,' he told Mannie.

'Spoilt little bugger!' his father spat out, whenever he perceived over-protectiveness on Camille's part.

Now, as Ralph stared at the MRI scan he felt his father beckoning.

'Come on my laddie, with all your fine ideas and your fancy education. Come and see what it is like to be trapped in a truly dark space and not be able to do a bloody thing about it!'

First it had been the pit. Thomas made his initial descent down the mineshaft in a state of total fear. He was shaking, he was afraid of wetting himself. There was nothing but darkness and then the veins of coal snaking through undressed stone, shining like threads of black diamonds in the intermittent half-light of a lamp. The cage rattled and shook; it made Thomas's bones ache and his teeth chatter.

Thomas wanted his mother. This seemed foolish to him,

he was not a mother's boy having been raised to be tough. Devoid of metaphors, of a language to sustain the mind through horrible events, he could only experience his descent down the mineshaft in a visceral kind of way. If the clarts of wet, sticky mud, swirling around his legs and up to his armpits, made him think of drowning he could not express it as such. All energy was steeled towards surviving the sense of claustrophobia, day after day, and Thomas soon discovered that drink was the best aid for his desired state of amnesia.

When Thomas talked about his childhood it was with an anger and bitterness that was directed towards Ralph. The frightened child had not been healed, but further brutalised by exposure to war. It had not occurred to Thomas that there could be worse places than the pit.

When Thomas volunteered to go to France he did not realise that the trenches were no different to the mines. It was like being in the pit, but the pit was both above and below the ground. The dugouts were a sea of blackened, swirling mud and the land above was darkened, charred. Thomas had visions of the heather moors back home, of the quiet retreats of country lanes and hedgerows. He vowed to never go back down the mine again, if he survived the war.

He didn't tell this part of the story to Ralph. The acknowledgement of the healing power of nature was a moment of self-disclosure that he kept hugged to himself, like an awkward secret. It was as though this self-knowledge had been won at such a high cost that he could not introduce natural pleasures into his son's life, in a simple way. Thomas Drew mainly took his walks on his own. He had spent years in the darkness in order to appreciate the flicker of sunlight on the Cheviot Hills; why should his son have it any easier?

History

Mannie methodically turns the pages of the album. She has come to know each photograph in detail.

There is a lengthy gap in time between the pictures of Thomas and Camille in their teens and a studio portrait of the couple as parents with baby Ralph.

'Look Ralph, what a beautiful christening gown. I always meant to ask your mother if it was a family heirloom.'

Mannie often wondered about the long childless interlude that preceded Ralph's birth. Had Camille tried for a baby before and, if so, why had it taken so long? It was a delicate area that she had not felt able to probe with her mother-in-law.

There are times when Ralph slips into the gap in time that Mannie questions. A raised voice is enough to set his mind careering in its direction, or any sort of crashing sound. Meal times are the worst. The rumble of the metal trolley being pushed across the ward floor distracts Ralph. The casters squeak on the linoleum; there is a cacophony of crashing stainless steel as plate-dividers; knives, spoons and forks slide about.

Ralph trembles. He hears the smashing of crockery and the hurling of knives and forks upon a stone floor. Then, a male voice in a rage – hoarse from screaming; a husky, rasping sound, like a jackdaw cawing from a rooftop.

'Bitch – always nagging! You blame me – don't you? You always blame me.'

A tiny bird is quivering in the corner of the kitchen. Ralph sees it now, perched by the stove. The creature's small breast heaves up and down with fear. Could this be the same bird that his father talked about when he was more level-headed, in a softer mood?

'War produces a strange climate of love,' Ralph's mother had told him, as though this was an explanation for everything. It was within this strange climate that his parents had met.

'Ah, a pretty bird sings,' a voice spoke from beneath the blood-soaked bandages. Only one eye was visible, an eye that focused on a petite young woman in nurse's uniform. The woman noted that the eye was dark, fiery, and that the soldier was lapsing in and out of consciousness. The woman appeared to the young man, who was barely older than a boy, as a mother bird gently flapping its wings – with a rustling of blue and white feathers.

'A drink – little bird,' he rasped, wondering, even in his confused state, at his choice of words. Then he opened his mouth, like a chick waiting for some morsel to be placed there.

The mother bird moved closer still. The man felt enveloped by the expanse of its wings and his head moved close to the creature's breast as it leant over to trickle water into his open mouth.

'What is your name?' the mother bird enquired.

'Thomas – Thomas Drew.'

'You need to sleep, Thomas. Shall I sing to you?'

The little bird sang a sweet, plaintive song and it seemed to Ralph's father that he had entered a magical space, despite the intrusion of physical pain and the sounds of human suffering. This experience was to haunt him for the rest of his life. Try as he might, he could not recapture the brief moment of ecstasy. He both loved and blamed Camille for this, for had she not seduced him with hope and desire? Had he not, for a few precious seconds, believed that he might be different, that life might be different; that he was capable of uttering soft words – discovering sensitivity hitherto unrevealed in his dark, miserable life?

Lucidity gave the small bird a name – Camille. She followed him back to England, after pleading with her guardian to allow her to marry. She was too young, Monsieur Berri argued and the man she wished to marry was from a different class, a foreign country. The Berri family feared for Camille but they didn't want to see her disappear like her mother before her. Better to give in, to know where she was living. Camille Dupont became the wife of Thomas Drew, an ex-colliery worker whose leg had been shot to bits in the war. He would never be able to work down the pit again and for this Thomas was grateful. He made his way as an odd job man, becoming a jack-of-all-trades. People thought him wily, resourceful, though given to brusqueness.

Camille found that her husband was not always harsh. There was a part of him that kept searching out the brief moment of their coming together. She found herself responding to this, never fully retreating from his drunkenness or angry outbursts.

'I saw the child in him, that was the hook,' she confided in Mannie, and Mannie felt that she understood this; that perhaps this was the way women always bonded with their men.

There were many occasions when Thomas fell into an inexplicable rage. It was impossible to pinpoint the focus: the pain in his leg, his childhood, the trauma of pit and trench? Even in the depths of this rage he knew that he was killing the songbird that had saved him, that its joyful outburst lay crushed within the limp body that lay smashed beneath his fists.

Camille tried not to blame Ralph's father for her first miscarriage. The doctor insisted that she had not lost the child because of the beating. She needed to believe this because she didn't want to hate her husband. It was true that he had been sorry; he had wept and felt wretched. For a while his anger was confined to words and inanimate objects. But there were several miscarriages preceding Ralph's birth years later. And when the child came Thomas showed no joy. Camille was dismayed by this indifference that bordered on resentment.

Mannie studies the photo.

'You were a sweet little baby Ralph, but you look troubled by the camera.'

Ralph is distracted, overwhelmed by the crashing of metal. His head is bobbing wildly.

'A ... Av ... Ave Marie,' he cries.

Mannie is pleased; she misinterprets Ralph's response as a sign that he recognises his mother in the photo. Ralph waits in anticipation – the brain synapse connected to memory has taken its own circuitous route and he expects the pink fuzzy object to sing to him.

Mannie doesn't understand this and is now focussed on encouraging Ralph to eat. She puts the album to one side and fetches a plate of food from the trolley.

'Afternoon tea – egg and bread dips. Let's see if it's softly boiled.'

Ralph moves his head to one side as Mannie attempts to spoon the runny yolk into his mouth. He is disappointed, though he cannot formulate or convey the feeling. If he could summon up the birdsong for himself it would give him some sense of ease, but it is always the same, stuck on his island with the incessant squawking of seagulls in the background.

Part Three

Paris 1889

Can-can

There is another world beyond the harshness of Parisian city life.

Elise Dupont and her friend Berthe walk the streets of the Montmartre district. The pair are at home within its carnivalesque atmosphere. We might find the two women, frozen in time, within one of Seurat's paintings. The circus is their favourite treat; they sit alert with excitement as a young woman gallops bareback around the ring. Berthe scans the ring in anticipation of a dark haired and moustached young man re-appearing. He wears yellow leggings – very tight fitting. Berthe digs Elise in the ribs, makes a sucking noise with an intake of breath. The pair rock with laughter.

Seurat does not paint this. Elise and Berthe are somehow a little too giddy. They duck and dive and bend double. For a painter who is drawn to the vertical the two friends are not a good subject, though he might note that the red feather in Elise's hat looks muddy against the purple felt.

It is the lure of gaslight that draws Seurat to the tree-lined avenues of Montmartre, where the bustle of human activity never ceases and darkness never truly descends. He has one goal in mind, to recreate this illuminated arena of sideshows and cabaret, this spectacle of sheer enjoyment.

Elise and Berthe *would* make Seurat their subject if they made his acquaintance. Outwardly he cuts an appealing figure, in his tailcoat and silk hat. He appears to belong to a homogenised group of bearded dandies. In reality, Seurat exists purely as an observer in the thick of this world, where the air is pungent with the smell of acetylene, fried potatoes and garlic sausages. The Montmartre district has a life force of its own, yet there is nothing about the atmosphere that truly seduces the young artist, apart from his mistress, Madeleine. He has only recently met the young model; an uneducated woman of twenty who has become his secret passion. Madeleine is hidden away from his family and friends, particularly his mother with whom he dines each evening.

Seurat has a deep affection for his mother but he doubts she will understand why this other woman has taken him unawares. He is bemused himself and his reason tells him that the liaison is strange – no one will understand the lure of his lover beyond her gaudy exterior, her over-ripe plumpness.

Seurat realises that it is the norm for his esoteric group of avant-garde contempories to pontificate on the stiffness of the bourgeoisie and the relaxed liberalism of the working class. It was fine to use a working class woman as a model from which to paint the human figure; but to be emotionally attached, to set up a home, to have children together – this was categorically not the norm.

In the external world Seurat remains the serious minded young man that others admire as a leader of a new avant-garde – the instigator of the neo-impressionist technique. He continues to take the sensuousness of the Montmartre experience and through his skill transforms it into a disciplined artistic form. All of this effervescence is to be resolved into verticals, curves and cylinders. The excitement of colour is to be mapped through a precise scientific law – Chevreul's law.

And what did Chevreul know of his follower, this mere youngster who was seventy-two years his junior? Several months ago, in this final year of his life, Chevreul had walked with his son Henri to observe the construction of the Eiffel Tower. The old man's eyes were dimmed with age, his mind confused. He may have walked past Seurat, unaware of his influence on the artist's decision to depict the tower with a shower of blue and orange dots.

Chevreul had once been sought out by Ingres, Delacroix and other eminent artists who heralded him as the technical prophet of Impressionism and Neo-impressionism. He had not sought this adulation. Chevreul's studies of colour vision and colour harmonies had been focused on one goal, to produce the best, the most exquisite tapestries, fabrics and carpets in his role as Director of Dyes for the Royal Manufacturers at Gobelins.

The reverence of artists was lost on Chevreul in his latter years. He confused the identities of individuals in his mind and the questions once posed by his eager followers became a vague memory. But the construction of the Tower was immediate for him; it was the last thing he enthused about to Elise Dupont before he died.

Elise has forgotten about his words of enthusiasm concerning the Tower. She felt sad about the old man's death, a little anxious about the future, but he had given her a good reference and she could always find work if she wanted to. It had been a strain at times, trying to meet her employer's standards. Now she is back to her comfortable self, free in a strange kind of way. Her evening out with Berthe is the highlight of the week.

The two women make their way home. Their ample figures are silhouetted against the gas-lit walls of narrow, bustling streets. They are a painting in the making.

'Next time we should go to the café-concert, so as I can dance the can-can.' Berthe announces.

Elise guffaws, as she lifts up her skirt to reveal thickened ankles that kick with jerky movements.

'I be as stiff as a wooden puppet!'

'You be out of practice, my girl. We got to do this more often.'

The two women might interest Seurat at this moment. If he retains the image in his mind he will draw two shadowy figures, rendering form by myriad edgeless marks. The women will be allowed less substance than if they were male figures. They are furtive, ghostly figures, filled in with darker tones, apart from the bright gleam of Elise's petticoat held high for all to see.

Secrets

Ruth is feeling tired. She has been on shift since early morning and the heat is draining her. She tugs at her white polyester uniform wishing that she were lying in her garden in a swimsuit.

Mannie looks across the room at Ruth and smiles wearily. The two women have developed a close friendship. This is partly due to the fact that Ruth comes from Mannie's home county, Northumberland. There is a shared experience of landscape and way of life.

'Don't you just long for a cold northern wind?' Ruth laughs, 'we're not used to this heat.'

She is helping Mannie to coax Ralph into eating his tea. Ralph's lack of interest in food is worrying Mannie. The consultant had explained to her the order in which the senses, the drives, gave up; informing her that the sex drive might 'hang around' for quite a while, depending on what medication was used and the rate at which the illness progressed. Mannie thought how this would have amused Ralph, that he might have depicted the notion of his sex drive 'hanging around' by way of a cartoon.

This is the kind of thing Mannie reflects upon when she writes in her notebook.

Sex. When I think about this now Ralph it is always to the early years of our relationship that I return. We never quite got it back together again in the same way after Sophia was born and I've started to wonder why? The consultant was anxious about explaining to me that you would regress but that your sex drive might remain for a while, or possibly be exaggerated by your state of mind. There was this silence in the room. He looked down at his desk; hands clasped together, waiting – waiting for me to respond. So I probed him some more. 'There might be some inappropriate behaviour,' he continued – and then more silence. Of course I knew what he meant Ralph, that all the secrets that we hold tight inside, enclosed in some private space in our minds, might come tumbling out in public by way of some masturbatory activity. I felt embarrassed, not by what he had just intimated, but by the thought of our private life being acted out in public. And then I felt afraid because I figured you might have secrets that we never shared, and I didn't want to know about that – not if you didn't really want me to.

But still I needed the warmth of your body next to mine at night. I clung onto this need and it feels, as your conscious interest in sex diminished, that I gradually became a child again – along with you. Play became touch and it was the opposite of what I had been afraid of because there were no words, there were no spoken fantasies. I did not mourn the passing of words as long as I could still have you close to me. This was probably naive of me; I should have known that with the death of words came the death of almost everything else.

Part of me came closer to understanding the

relationship between Camille and your father, because I had to take the weight of your aggression. This was such a heavy weight Ralph, but I knew it came from a hurt, confused space in you. You had never been aggressive with me before and it was strange coping with such an unfamiliar impulse, trying to maintain tenderness when you had verbally or physically hurt me – and I realised that Camille had endured a similar scenario with your father most of her adult life.

After the squabbles, the hassle of trying to encourage you to do the simplest of things, we tumbled into bed exhausted. Sometimes this took half the night. Like a hyperactive child you mentally and physically ran circles around me for hours. But then it was silence – bliss. You would fell asleep, the stress of illness removed from your face – strangely youthful. I preferred this 'quiet zone' to the one the doctors promised if we increased your medication – the 'medical cosh' as Sophia called it.

I sensed the child in you – I felt like a child myself – we were two orphans in exile from the world that most people inhabit. This is the bond we make when we fall in love – just like Camille said – and you have remained my child long after you ceased to be a husband. And that part of you I will never abandon Ralph – never.

Mannie isn't sure that keeping the notebook is helping her. It's as though she is probing her relationship with Ralph in a way that she didn't do before the illness. What would Ralph feel if he could read her thoughts and is this what he meant by urging her to remember the precious things?

Abandonment

Mannie wishes that she had listened more attentively when Ralph tried to explain to her why Seurat could have painted what it is like to be trapped inside a confused mind. It was all do with light and shade and a technique called chiaroscuro.

During the early years of the illness she was bemused that Ralph could go on constructing ideas when everyday life was falling into disarray. It was as though by a sheer act of will he had cordoned off part of his brain, the most precious part. To hang with the fact that he forgot the names of friends and colleagues, set knives and forks the wrong way round, left pans to boil dry and mislaid his keys. These small confusions were the early warning signs of the illness, but Ralph could still be eloquent and it was easy to think that there was nothing of a serious nature wrong. Then – suddenly – the silent and invisible attack on Ralph's verbal skills gained force.

Ralph realised that he had done badly on the verbal test. It was the speed with which he had been asked to answer the questions. He had looked at the simple pictures, recognised what they represented, but failed to recollect the correct word. His mind was in a fog. The humiliation was doubled when the consultant relayed the answers back to him and the words slotted back into place, so simply and clearly. Ralph felt as if his voice were suddenly speaking from outside of him. It was as though his private mental space had been stolen. Despite the internal turmoil, he smiled and apologised.

It was painful for Ralph to feel anger and irritation when he was still in connection with the fact that his natural disposition was to be calm and polite. Even now, as he sits huddled on his island, he is aware that there is a huge part of himself missing and that this is the reason for his anguish; an anguish that causes him to sob inconsolably, or to lash out in anger and frustration.

The sound of the crying and frustration invades Ruth's head. It is not only Ralph's distress that rattles round in her mind, long after she has left the ward. All of the patients have some form of dementia. She spends her day in the midst of a communal confusion that is impossible to contain.

Now Amy has wandered off to the other side of the ward, dragging her feet in slippers that are worn down in a crease at the back. The slippers are a misshapen mess and Ruth can see that Amy is leaking and that the slippers will need to be washed once again. Not all of the nurses are so vigilant; hard pressed for time and somewhat traumatised by this harsh presentation of what could be their own future, Amy's slippers are last on the list of problems to be attended to.

Mannie puts Ralph's meal to one side, wondering whether to follow Amy and attempt some form of assistance. She is still trying to figure out her annoyance and thinks perhaps it's because this shell of a woman seems to understand some of Ralph's incoherence. Mannie isn't clear why she surmises this, deciding it may simply be an assumption she has made based on her reading of a look of sadness in Ralph and Amy's eyes; a desolate kind of sadness that Mannie fantasizes as a chain of empathy between them.

Once, she had asked Ruth about Amy's background. Ruth had thought for a while before replying – not wanting to betray a patient confidentiality.

'Amy was admitted when her husband could no longer cope. He was a nice old boy, in his eighties. They were both retired schoolteachers. Can you imagine it, our frail little Amy controlling a whole class of children?'

Mannie had tried to visualise a youthful Amy, to put flesh on the starkly delineated cheekbones and the fragile, gnarled sticks that now served as arms and legs.

'No, I can't imagine it. Are there any photos?'

'A photo?' Ruth pondered. 'No, I don't think so. Amy's husband died soon after she was admitted. There are no living relatives. Well – none that seem to care.'

Mannie had felt disturbed. Suddenly, Amy didn't seem quite so irritating, but now she had become a symbol of abandonment and the symbolic weight of this was more threatening than mere irritation. She found her annoyance with Amy increased rather than dissipated and each new visit provoked a stronger response than the one before.

Mannie pretends to fuss with the rejected meal as her eyes follow Amy's shuffling walk. It has suddenly occurred to her that she doesn't want Ralph to feel empathy for this frail creature, and that this translated means that she doesn't want Ralph to feel abandoned.

'No! no! no!' Ralph screamed, rolling his hands over his bowed head, when Mannie had tried to explain that she needed respite care.

Ralph had defied all expectations, outstripping the original prognosis of six years from 'start to finish' as the consultant had bluntly put it. Six years had become seven, then eight, then nine, ten and eleven. It was only in the twelfth year of the illness that things reached breaking point. Sophia, Mark and their daughter Kerry had come to stay over Christmas, as Ralph was far too ill to leave the house.

'You can't go on like this,' Sophia had insisted, after witnessing one of her father's rages. The statement had given Mannie permission to admit that she could no longer cope. It was true that Social Services had been helping, taking some of the physical strain, but they couldn't be around twenty-four hours a day. Ralph seemed to save his more hostile moods for when they were alone together and Mannie knew that it was because the impossibility of reaching the part of himself that was missing was more painful in her presence.

That was a strange conundrum Ralph – one that I had to work out. What were you seeing when I stood before you – sharing in, but not fully experiencing, in the way you were forced to, the terrible humiliation? Is this what you meant when you tried to explain to me about painting; how normally you would begin by defining the light patches, but that the shadows were taking over and what would happen when the shadows no longer gave off any light? Because, you assured me, they did give off light in Seurat's paintings. I remember you saying that there was no such thing as total shadow – only gradations of tone.

Where are you now Ralph? What would you tell me about this world of chiaroscuro, this world of light and shade? Does true darkness exist? Is black a colour that we can totally inhabit or is there light at the edges? These are the sorts of questions that fill my mind now Ralph and I wish that we could talk, talk like we used to – but with a change of emphasis. You always posed the questions and I listened but not in a particularly interactive way. Now I'm thinking – was this because you were more powerful, more knowledgeable? Was it because I have a tendency to be mentally lazy? And what is happening to me now Ralph? All sorts of questions burn like fire in my mind. They give me no peace.

Chiasma

There is a painting on the wall in Ralph's attic depicting his father. Mannie had not recognised it as such, not until Ralph tried to explain. Black lines cross the page – a tangle of barbed wire. The lines are criss-crossed with red and orange explosions of colour.

'Chiasma!' Ralph had cried excitedly, rocking to and fro.

'What is it Ralph?' Mannie asked, knowing that a straightforward explanation would not be forthcoming.

Ralph's mind seemed to lock on single words, not in an arbitrary way but with a stringent condensation that was difficult to unravel. Mannie felt she ought to know the meaning of the word, recognise the meaning of the meaning. It was like a strange game of free association.

'Chiasma!' Ralph cried out again, scribbling furiously with an orange crayon.

Here was a point of fury with his father. His father had lied to him. No-man's-land was not simply composed of black. No – Ralph had experienced something else, and that experience was sparking out of the end of the crayon. Ralph did not know how to verbally express what he had seen, as he cowered behind a rock on Blue-Grey Island, that morning.

The sound of Mannie dropping a tray in the kitchen had startled him, forced him to run for cover. A light – a fantastic light – a shattered rainbow spilling its colours like shards of glass. This is what he had seen.

'It is the explosion of mines,' a voice whispered beside him, 'see how they explode in an arc.'

Ralph felt the ground beneath him rumble and shake as the flames leapt like giant snake tongues, spewing out clouds of dust and smoke. Then the flash of gunfire, a bursting of shells, split the arc of light asunder.

'Ah!' Ralph called out, causing Mannie to abandon the fallen tray and come running in.

'It's only the tea tray, Ralph. Nothing to be afraid of.'

'See the rainbow of light,' the other voice whispered, 'and below us, look at this uncanny river of mud.'

Ralph felt a powerful tugging at the top of his head. He recognised this as the scramble of brain synapses desperately trying to impose order on his unruly memory. Ralph could feel the pressure exerted by his brain as it prized apart the prefix 'un' from 'canny'.

'Canny, canny, canny!' he chuckled. This had been a favourite word of his father's.

'That's a canny little dress,' he would say to Camille on his softer days.

Ralph looked down and saw that his feet were balanced on duckboards, placed over a muddy crater. The crater was filled to the brim with water.

'The fragments of light have fallen into the water,' the voice whispered into his ear.

It was true. Ralph could see that the water was a swirl of metallic colours. His ears were buzzing and the sound echoed in his head with a continuous droning. Then he looked up, slowly, warily. High in the sky, he saw a flock of messenger birds, their wings a shiny grey against the softer, muted grey of the clouds. They have wings of steel, Ralph thought to himself, strangely satisfied that something had conveyed itself to him in words.

Later in the day he drew. This was an activity that Mannie encouraged because Ralph seemed more focused on externalising his thoughts when he was drawing.

Mannie reached for the dictionary. She knew this would probably look strange to an outsider but Ralph frequently threw words out into the ether that she didn't know the exact meaning of. At least this one was in English.

'*Chiasma* – a cross-shaped mark,' she read, turning to Ralph. 'Or maybe a crossing – over point? No – more a point of intersection?'

Ralph wasn't really listening, as he was absorbed in drawing furiously. His father had not told him, as a boy, about the rainbow light and how it contained the energy and the anger of thousands of men; that it had shattered into an infinitesimal number of pieces and fallen to earth. His father had one of the pieces embedded in his heart and throughout Ralph's childhood he had raged with the pain of it. Ralph reaches into his father's heart; the crayon is a scalpel that searches out flesh. And the flesh of his father is not the blackened flesh of a tyrant but the red, weeping flesh of a human being who has been brutalised as a child. What is Ralph to do with this knowledge, trapped in a mind that feels and thinks in its own way, but that can no longer convey thoughts to another?

Mannie is still reading the dictionary.

'Guess what Ralph; *chiaroscuro* is listed straight above *chiasma*. Now that's what you would call serendipity.'

Mannie is all ready for a discussion; one of those discussions Ralph would have loved to enjoy in their previous life.

Ennui

Mannie wonders if it is sheer boredom that has sparked off her phase of mental questioning. She asks herself how she would describe her state of mind in the years prior to Ralph's illness and decides that a degree of calm complaisance sums it up.

What would you say about this Ralph? Perhaps that I was a happy child, the product of an uneventful childhood and that I had carried the calmness over into adulthood. You would say the words kindly, without a hint of criticism so why do I feel critical towards myself? Did my calmness come out of a lack of relationship? Remember – I had my mother to myself for five years. My father remained a distant hero until the war ended. Some might think that this amounted to deprivation but it meant that I lived in a conflict free world as far as adult relationships were concerned. You loved my mother Ralph, my warm, stoical mother. Surely she must have experienced great pain; the hardships that war inflicts, the separation from my father, but all I can remember of this time is growing up within the security of our extended family. And when my father returned their fractured lives somehow melded together without any obvious strain.

I ask myself now whether your imaginative mind was the

product of a great struggle to survive a difficult childhood. Did you have to dig deeper into yourself, create another world to slip into when the going got tough? What do I know of harsh words and brutality – I who was the apple of my father's eye?

I was fortunate Ralph but perhaps unprepared for the ups and downs of life. I disregarded the value of a good education, leaving school at sixteen even though I could have stayed on. I wanted to be with my friends, to go off to secretarial college. I was given a choice. But you had to struggle and if it hadn't been for Camille's determination your father would never have allowed you to take up your scholarship.

And so I ended up in administration, working in a university rather than attending one. At least I had a sense of being around learning and sometimes, in my lunch-break, I would wander over to the library and browse through the books. I think this was more to do with the pull of the opposite sex than learning. The atmosphere was exciting to me; it was like skating round the periphery of a world that I could not be fully part of. I used to fantasize that one of the students would ask me out – preferably one of the romantic ones; a student of literature and poetry. Not wanting to appear stupid I read a bit and found that I quite enjoyed it, but I was secretive about this activity.

I have been watching the magpies in the garden – the way they love to steal bright objects. Is this what I'm like Ralph, a bird that collects little sparkly nuggets of information; small treasures that I store away? I think this is how I got by on the occasions I had to be in academic circles with you. I learnt how to chip in intelligently every now and then, enough not to be sitting there like a silent buffoon, but never so much as to compromise you or myself.

Have I been like a magpie round you? Remember the 'big discussion' after we got married as to whether I wanted to take up further education? I was reading quite a lot at the time, mainly novels. I told you that I couldn't see the necessity for formal study when we wanted to start a family. Now I think, did you want that for me or for you? Did my passivity annoy you?

My nest of goodies suddenly seems very full: years and years worth of silent thoughts, taken from here, there and everywhere. The thoughts spill out of me, so many unresolved questions, the beginnings of ideas that never got worked through.

Do I believe in God? Now there's a big one. I feel anger Ralph; is God a good receptacle for this? I've never felt a genuine relationship with a higher power as you do. Prayer, as you know, does not come easy to me. When I try, and I do try now in my desperation, I might as well be listening to the sound of leaves rustling in the wind. Where is this voice that you can hear?

Do you still believe in a benevolent higher power and if you don't I wonder when your belief slipped away? Sometimes I feel there is a swaying rope bridge over a deep cavern and that you are at one end and I am at the other. And I know that you have walked across this bridge, negotiated its perilous swaying and caught many glimpses of the cavernous depths below. If I could walk the same brave steps I would know the answer to some of these questions, I would know what decimates belief and what strengthens it.

But I am the spoilt child Ralph and it was ever the way that if one of us had to make this journey it would fall to you.

The Cave

God lives in a cave on Blue-Grey Island. This is a secret location but Ralph has thought for a while that there are others who have rumbled the mystery. He first had his suspicions when he came across a print of Seurat's painting of an imposing rock face, *The Bec Du Hoc, Grandcamp*.

Ralph kept a copy of the painting, torn from an art book, in his 'important information' box in the attic. The box is concealed behind an old filing cabinet, no one knows of its existence – not even Mannie. Ralph decided that the rock was a landmark signifying the highest point on his island. The rock is an immense mass and Ralph felt the weight of it bearing down on the sea below. Above the rock flew five messenger birds.

Ralph was afraid of the messenger birds. These creatures were even more threatening than the crows. A messenger bird was capable of pulling him from his chair and depositing him on the island. Ralph looked at the rock and felt that it was moving, that some intense energy force was pulsating from within the static mass, causing it to judder. The rock leans towards the right of the picture frame. Seurat's brushwork had been caught up in the power of the diagonal. Ralph sensed God leaning over with stretched and elongated limbs. He felt that two hands would surely push out from the top of the rock releasing white doves into the sky.

'The doves of peace,' a voice whispered, and Ralph wondered why his father had taken to talking so quietly.

'What if God breathes?' Ralph enquired.

'The sea will no longer be calm,' the voice replied.

'I thought as much,' Ralph murmured, agitated now. 'I must tell Mannie to prepare for shipwreck.'

Mannie couldn't understand it, why Ralph insisted on packing boxes of 'rations'.

'Why do we need to do this Ralph, are you afraid of going hungry?'

Ralph shook his head in irritation. Even his father understood the importance of rations. Hadn't he described to Ralph the contents of his kit bag?

'A packet of Woodbines,' Ralph insisted.

Mannie had no idea where she was supposed to get these and besides Ralph had never smoked.

'Dried soup!' Ralph added gleefully. This was an excellent idea.

Mannie struggled on these occasions, half wondering whether to go along with Ralph's requests, or whether to try and rationalise. Rationalising never really worked; Ralph would become distressed and angry and then there was no pacifying him. Mannie hated this, the notion of trying to pacify Ralph. This, she felt, is what strips away his dignity.

Ralph knew that it was pointless to resist the journey. Now that he realised that God lived on the island he was a little less afraid. Would he be allowed to meet God, he wondered, to see him face to face? Even now he remembers the last leg of the journey.

The messenger birds had come for their final offensive – the mission to capture him – though others would say he had simply fallen, in fact – this was written on his hospital admissions report. No one had seen the birds pulling him mercilessly from his chair, how he had stumbled and crashed to the floor in an attempt to escape the rush of air from flapping wings and the piercing pain of being pecked at by their sharp beaks. He had been admitted '… *with cuts and lacerations*,' the report stated.

It had been a chaotic event marked by a great deal of pushing and pulling. Family members lost their recognisable form as they became messenger birds. He was forcibly lifted, carried away – dazed on arrival. God did not come out to meet him. Ralph is still waiting to look upon the face of God. But an angel was sent ahead to greet him, a floating white presence, which continues to protect him in his frightened state.

The angel is called Ruth.

Black Holes

Mannie is getting edgy. She is thinking about her diary, almost missing the morning routine of sitting at her corner of the desk in the attic. She has come to enjoy this time of reflection, feeling it brings her closer to Ralph. Closer than she feels now, uncomfortably perched on a hard hospital chair. She longs for them both to be sprawled on the sag-bag armchairs at home, with the wood-burning stove crackling and burning.

I sometimes think that this is the conversation I'm having with you and it is also the conversation that I can never have with you – that I let you have all the words Ralph and now this responsibility has passed to me. How strange it is that through your silence I am forced to use words and I wonder now how you experienced my silence?

A few days ago Mannie had visited the local library and picked out a book on black holes. She was drawn to the picture on the book's cover – a swirling blue mass set against the backdrop of a dark, star-studded sky.

Mannie wishes she had brought the book with her; the cover is similar to some of Ralph's paintings and she feels sure that it would stimulate a spark of recognition. Ralph had been researching the composition of dark matter before his illness. One of the theories that captivated him was the possibility that dark matter might be partially composed of black holes. Mannie's understanding of this is very sketchy, but she has to accept that her limited knowledge now far exceeds any information that Ralph can recall.

Ralph has shown no interest in his tea; the remains of the boiled egg lays cold on the plate. Mannie is desolate – a sensation of sheer emptiness suddenly hits her. She is dizzy from the heat, from the plain awfulness of the situation. Her worst fear is that Ralph is slipping away from her, that he already exists in a world far removed from any place that she can reach. It all feels so eerie. Ralph's face is translucent; his eyes stare into space and Mannie is certain that this is not a vacant stare but the look of a human being who sees a world different to the one that she confidently sees.

Mannie thinks once again of the library book and tries to recollect what she had written down the previous day. Her mind is working rapidly – making new notes.

I want to tell you about something Ralph, a thought I had the other day that caused me pain. I suddenly realised that you had mapped it all out – before you began to 'lose' your mind – what this illness would mean for you. How terrifying that must have been!

You told me that you were afraid that you would reach a space that represented limbo and that within this space you would lose all knowledge and sense of endings. When this happened the terror and the pain of the illness would be a constant within your mind. You wouldn't be able to get behind it to a sense of the past and you wouldn't be able to think forward in time in order to imagine the pain ending. I blanked you out, too afraid to imagine what the words might mean.

This book I'm reading, it is full of equations – the sort I would pull faces over when I used to type up stuff for you! Those beautiful building blocks of physics were a fascination for you but I could never follow even the simplest ones. But the words I can grasp at and the words interest me.

I wish I could talk to you about this Ralph; it's as though I've been pushed off the edge of inertia into a sea of questions. It began to occur to me that the reason you painted all those swirling masses was because in some way you were still thinking about black holes.

I have been trying to give this some attention, to sharpen my understanding of what a black hole represents, because I know this wouldn't have been a vague concept for you as it might be for me, but would have been based on all you had specifically known and thought about.

What does a black hole represent? Essentially an object with a gravitational field so strong that nothing, not even light, can escape if it comes within the gravitational pull. A human body would be torn apart into tiny pieces, so strong is the gravitational force.

Remember how you used to draw cartoons to explain difficult theories? In my mind's eye I can see a little stick person hovering near the entrance to the black hole. The stick person tentatively puts out its foot to the edge of a clearly delineated line. There is a signpost pointing towards the line that reads 'Danger – event horizon circumference'. Step the wrong side of this and you are sucked into the black hole's force field. The stick person decides to ignore the sign and pieces of his body fly in a thousand different directions as he crosses the line. But something remains: a tiny black speck, a mind.

The tiny black speck is pulled down a long tunnel and as it looks up from the tunnel the universe, the starry sky, is compressed into an area no larger than a dinner plate. As it descends the hole the colours of the stars change; yellow stars become green then blue. Time imperceptibly slows down – the mind has entered another time zone, another universe. On the other side of the event horizon wars have been fought, generations have grown old and died. History has unravelled centuries of stories as the mind floats down the space tunnel in what feels like seconds.

How am I doing Ralph? I see you giving a simple explanation of a black hole with all the excitement that went into those descriptions, but I never really felt the excitement before now. My responses have always been a little tame and my excitement more connected to everyday things. Like this morning, a baby robin hopped out in front of me as I was taking the rubbish out and it filled my heart with a sense of glee. Netta always said that robins were a sign of good luck.

Ralph, some of your paintings look like giant egg timers. In this book I'm reading it says that a black hole is a 'wormhole' connecting two universes. The wormhole does look like an egg timer or a funnel. What is it like, being sucked into another universe? It feels scary to me, knowing that you are being pulled towards a place where familiarity is turned on its head, where you disappear from the view of everyone and everything you ever cared about, only to be born anew in a strange and far off land.

If Ralph could answer Mannie he would explain that there is a kind of wormhole called an Einstein-Rosen bridge that can connect different areas of our same universe; that it is not necessarily correct to interpret another region of space-time as another universe. He does after all keep bumping into his father in no-man's-land. It seems to Ralph that Blue-Grey Island is connected to the world that he used to inhabit by a very particular wormhole, one that has not been discovered. But the guiding principle is the same – there is no way back.

Sophia

Sophia parks in the drive and lets out a huge sigh of relief to be home. The school run has exhausted her.

'Phew! Let's get out of this car Kerry – I'm positively cooked.'

Young Kerry, red faced and sitting like a limp rag doll in the backseat, suddenly springs to life.

'Cook-a-doodle-do!' she announces, in a voice that is pitched an octave above mere talking level.

'I want the paddling pool out. I want to swim!'

'Ok, Ok. I might be tempted to come in myself.'

Sophia is slightly pre-occupied with the thought of her mother visiting Ralph today. She tries to conjure up an image of her father as he used to be; her gentle, introspective father but it's no use. All she can visualise is a broken man; a pale, tense face framed by wisps of white hair. Sophia recollects how she had attempted to wash and cut her father's hair during her last visit.

'Come on Pops,' she had jollied along. 'We don't want you looking like a mad professor – do we?'

Her mother had winced at the insensitive choice of words. There is an ongoing tension between Sophia and Mannie; their ways of coping are at variance. Sophia watches her mother and finds the attempts to remain 'normal' with Ralph increasingly annoying.

'Can't she see that my father has changed, everything has changed?' she complains to her partner Mark.

'You can't blame her. Imagine how it would be for you if it were I in that state?' Mark had reasoned with her, conscious that one of his roles in life had become that of umpire between Sophia and her mother.

'You're already demented – I wouldn't have to make much of an adjustment – would I?'

Sophia sometimes wonders where she gets her caustic sense of humour – certainly not from her parents. She knows that she is overtly cynical, downright coarse at times, but she can't help herself. This has always been her way of surviving in the world. Her ancestry is hidden from her; nothing can be traced from her grandmothers Camille and Netta for they were both gentle, self-effacing women. Sophia's veins pulsate with the life force of three generations of women she has no knowledge of; Elise, Marie and Catherine Dupont.

Little Kerry is in fact the image of her great-great-grandmother Catherine Dupont, with her dark brown eyes and copper curls. Kerry prefers this description of her hair as copper because she has a sneaking suspicion that it is really closer to red – or worse still, orange.

'Not carrot – copper!' she hisses at the boys who tease her in the playground. She is well known for her temper tantrums. Kerry wonders if her hair changes colour when this happens. She practices getting angry in front of a mirror in the hope that she can catch a glimpse of this strange phenomenon. She has heard herself described as a little girl with 'attitude'.

Sophia remembers her mother saying this. 'Attitude' was one of those contemporary words her mother had latched onto. She's just high-spirited, Sophia muses, as Kerry sprays her with the hosepipe.

'My turn!' Sophia shrieks, grabbing the hosepipe from Kerry and chasing her round the garden. 'Raucous – that's what we are, raucous.'

Sophia doesn't really understand why the antipathy towards her mother has escalated. Admittedly, their relationship had always been a little tense, but she feels this stronger wave of negativity must surely have to do with the stress of her father becoming so ill.

'Right – that's enough Kerry, I'm going to make us a cold drink.'

'Can we have ice lollies?'

'Ok – ice lollies it is.'

Sophia sits down in the kitchen, waiting to get her breath back. Her hands instinctively cup her stomach. Can't do any harm, she reasons, it's just a little run round. She had used the pregnancy test a week ago, cried out excitedly as the marker indicated positive. 'We've done it,' she told Mark, 'we've broken the family spell.' It was a secret she'd decided to relish for a little while. She plans to tell her mother soon, perhaps even today after Mannie returns home from visiting the hospital. Her mother would be pleased; of course she'd be pleased. So – why the delay?

To banish any hint of anger. This is what Sophia has deduced. She doesn't want to intimate that this baby is a triumph – against what? Being an only child? How she had hated being an only child, cooped up at Grange Farm, with no playmates close by. It wasn't as though it had even been a real farm, she had grumbled, with chickens, cows and horses for company. 'Why?' she had asked her mother, 'why can't I have a brother or sister?'

'It was not to be,' her mother had told her. 'Of course we wanted a brother or sister for you but it just didn't happen.'

Little Sophia had wondered about this. It would have been so much fun having someone to play with. When she was four she invented an imaginary friend. His name was Skipper; he was half way between a dog and a little boy. Sophia reckoned, when she thought back on this, that it was all part of her being used to being number one. 'Here Skipper,' she called and her imaginary friend ran at her heels. She was always in command.

'Do you remember how Skipper got the blame for everything?' her father had laughed one day as they were reminiscing.

'Mm ... like the time I decided to dismantle your astronomy gear in the attic?'

'Oh dear, I did get cross with you about that. I shouldn't have done, it was only a child's natural curiosity.'

Sophia moves quickly from the kitchen stool to the freezer. She can feel the tears welling up. It is hard to take in the fact that her father no longer recognises her. 'He must be so lonely,' she talks to herself. 'I wonder, does he have an imaginary friend?' She is still pondering this question when Mark returns from work.

'Do you think dad has an imaginary friend to keep him company?' she asks.

Mark stops stirring his cup of coffee and thinks. 'Well that would be God wouldn't it?' he half-laughs, flipping the spoon into the sink. 'I'm sorry Sophia, I didn't mean that to sound cruel.'

'No – I know, and anyway I sort of hope that it's true.'

Sophia sighs. She had engaged in so many heated debates with her father on this issue. Well – the heat had been mainly on her side, she recalls. She bites her bottom lip as she recollects attacking her father's allegiance to the Catholic Church, how she had railed against its hierarchies and dogmas – its scandals and cover-ups.

Ralph had reasoned with her that this happened within every religion and every facet of human life; the abuse of power was not just confined to the Catholic Church. In his view this did not mean that belief should be abandoned or that debate and discussion could never really achieve progress.

Sophia had her doubts – always coming up with examples of the ways in which fundamentalism impinged on secular life. Yet she knew that by his example her father was not a fundamentalist. The belief in a personal God seemed to keep him anchored – prayer gave him comfort and assurance. Seen in this context did she have a right to question her father's faith – and did she in any true way even understand it?

'I need some quiet time,' she tells Mark, 'can you take Kerry to the park for a little while.'

'Sure – come on piglet – first one to the car gets an ice cream!'

Sophia wonders if it's the heat, or the start of morning sickness, that is making her feel nauseous and tired. She decides to rest in bed but within a few minutes of lying down is unsettled. A heavy sensation bores into her eyes and closing them brings no relief. She sits up and smoothes her forehead, which has creased into a frown as a memory begins to coalesce.

'The wardrobe … the wardrobe …' she mutters, climbing out of bed and dragging a stool from under the dressing table to the wardrobe door.

The stool wobbles as Sophia clambers to reach the top shelf. She pulls out a heavy cardboard box, cursing as she lifts it down before toppling back onto the bed. The lid is fastened with a piece of discoloured elastic. Sophia smiles, thinking it is typical of her to have not used ribbon because it would have been too feminine a gesture. The box contains old letters, school reports, birthday cards and a piece of faded white lace.

The white lace is the remains of Sophia's confirmation garb. She places the veil on her head pulling the lace down over her eyes.

'Rosary beads,' she mumbles, 'they must be in here somewhere. I can't possibly remember the words of the rosary.'

The beads are found – ten small stones – pearly and lavender blue in colour, strung on a delicate gold chain. The chain makes a circle no bigger than a child's wrist. There is a shorter length of chain joined to the circle by a tiny, sacred heart. A solitary bead is positioned mid-centre in the length of chain, and at the very end a gold crucifix.

Sophia remembers her father buying the beads as a replacement for the plainer wooden ones she had been given, by one of the nuns, during confirmation classes. Her attendance at church lapsed a couple of years after her confirmation, when she reached a point of rebellion in her teenage years. Her father did not stand in the way of this, explaining to her that religion without the felt presence of God in one's life was meaningless – that he had hoped to provide her with a structure, a springboard to belief, but that she must choose to dive in at her own behest.

Sophia never dived in. She questions now whether she had even so much as got her feet wet. What to do with the emotions of loss and loneliness, the grief and distress connected to her father's illness?

The rosary beads feel warm in the palm of her hand. She rubs the tiny gold cross at the end of the strand between her fingertips and attempts to recollect Sister Anne's instruction in confirmation class.

The image of Sister Anne has stayed firm in Sophia's memory. The nun had been young and pretty, a visual distraction from the boredom of class. Sophia had committed the irreverent act of mentally removing the voluminous folds of black drapery from Sister Anne's body. The nun's habit was then replaced with the latest fashion statement; much in the way that Sophia had dressed the paper cut-out-dolls she had played with as a child. She smiles now as she recollects the Goth stage of her early teens – thinking that it was all a bit of a parody of the dark austerity, of the nun's garb, she had witnessed as an impressionable child. Then she remembers how the accessorising with ornate crucifixes had totally bemused her father, and feels a twinge of guilt.

'The rosary is divided into fifteen decades,' Sister Anne had informed the motley group of children.

Sophia had been spared attendance at convent school and remembers her scathing attitude towards the other children in the confirmation class, who had not enjoyed such a 'lucky escape'. Her parents had believed that her personality would thrive in the smaller classes of the local private school, but she wonders now if this had only added to a sense of insularity.

Her mind is confused as she attempts to remember the fifteen decades. It was all to do with the mysteries of redemption based on events, such as 'the annunciation' or 'the agony in the garden'.

'The fifteen decades are divided into groups of five within the three mysteries,' Sister Anne had continued, her eyes piercing with earnestness.

Sophia can't remember the details; she had not been concentrating the first time, so intent had she been on conjuring the nun's new wardrobe.

'Found you!' she cries with delight as she retrieves a faded leaflet from the box entitled, 'How to Say the Rosary'.

Sophia studies the leaflet. There are The Joyful Mysteries, The Sorrowful Mysteries and The Glorious Mysteries. The memories start to return of the Holy days, the feast days, the Advents and the Epiphanies, the Resurrections and the Ascensions, the Coronations and the Assumptions, year after year after year. Sophia feels drowsy surveying this calendar of ritual, faith and belief.

She lies down on the bed and shuts her eyes, closing her palm around the rosary beads.

'Dear God, please take care of my dad and if he can't improve release him from his suffering. Amen.'

She feels about five and realises this isn't much of a prayer, but it will have to do.

Do You Remember?

Mannie can see that Ralph is becoming tired. His body is limp and his head hangs down. There are traces of egg and saliva at the edges of his mouth. She leans over to wipe away the frothy, yellow stain and then changes her mind. Soon Ralph will nod off. Mannie wonders where he goes to when this happens; what becomes of Ralph in his dreams? She thinks there is probably some research project going on somewhere, trying to define all of this, but she is glad that her husband is not part of it.

I dreamt about Netta, just this morning,' she whispers. 'I was a child again and we were walking by Rothberry Moors. My feet were bare and I paddled in a stream with brightly coloured fish. The fish nibbled my toes. It tickled!'

Mannie furtively scans the ward, embarrassed that she is relating to a dream. Amy is staring at her, an uncomfortable stare. She goes to babble something but Mannie resolutely turns away, hoping that Amy will be occupied when Sophia comes on Sunday. Sophia always engaged with Amy, attempting to bring her into their family grouping.

'Why not,' she had protested. 'Amy gets no visitors and she's more responsive towards me than Dad.'

Sophia's prickly tongue hurts Mannie.

I keep trying to work out what is happening for Sophia. I sometimes think that Mark and Sophia's wedding was the first day of my really accepting that you were truly gone from us. It's hard – watching the video. You look so dignified with your hair swept back, wearing that lovely suit Sophia insisted on buying for you. Even I look presentable, though I hated the way the hairdresser piled my hair up. Not my style Ralph!

But the speeches – I can hear the strain in your voice as you struggled to speak a few well-rehearsed words. It must have been so hard for you to concentrate. And Sophia, how beautiful she looked. Where do her wild looks come from Ralph? Not me, that's for sure! She has always been a little wild. I remember the first time she removed her shoes as a baby. There was a defiant gleam in her eyes – what a game that became. Can you remember how she used to run barefoot in the garden, the tantrums we'd have if we tried to get her to put shoes on? It shouldn't have really mattered, but we never did clear the garden and I was afraid of her hurting herself. Do you remember the spring she fell into a patch of stinging nettles and we rowed – so unusual for you and I – and you scythed the nettles down and every spring thereafter?

Why is she so angry with me?

Do you think it was too isolated at home? I don't think I realised at the time that it might be lonely for her. She had my attention and I thought that was enough, that we would be close like Netta and myself or you with Camille. I should have known when she created Skipper that something was amiss.

'Don't tell mummy our secret,' she announced to Skipper when she knew I was within earshot.

But there were other children around some of the time

Ralph. Remember the Wilkinsons, they often called in on a weekend with their boys. Tony Wilkinson, your colleague and dear friend who died so young of cancer – and his wife Mary. I don't think Mary was very keen on me; I had the feeling that she found us Luddite, not what you would expect from a scientist and his family.

But Sophia really liked their visits. Remember that little tea set we bought her, how she would always get it ready only to find that the boys weren't that interested. She soon grew out of that though. One day the boys brought a box of lego with them and that transformed her playtimes. You were quick to spot how creatively her mind worked and from that time on she never picked out girl's stuff from the toyshop.

Did I feel that I'd lost her then? Maybe – I think I was a little jealous and that's when the urge to have another baby got really strong.

Oh how I wanted that other baby!

Do you remember Ralph, do you remember, do you remember?

Part Four

Hot Soup

Elise Dupont never made it to the café-concert. Her fate is sealed with Seurat's.

'I be feeling unwell.'

'A drop of absinthe in warm water mends anything!' Berthe snaps.

Elise is slumped on her bed; her pudgy hands knead the grimy bedcover as though it is a giant piece of dough. Berthe sits, straddling a wooden chair. A knowing look flits across her face.

'There be all kinds of illnesses going about; people dropping like flies they say. Won't be room to bury us all soon!'

Elise groans; drops of sweat run down the creases in her cheeks. 'You be making me feel worse! Fetch that drink.'

Marie stands in the doorway, her expression a mixture of curiosity and insolence. 'I be feeling ill too – I need some of Berthe's medicine.'

Marie has spent most of the day arranging and re-arranging the doll's house and is now bored. Part of her misses Catherine. It is a cold March day, a day for sitting by the stove – playing, but there is no one to play with. It is seven months since her daughter went to live with the Berri household and Catherine has visited but once. Marie had thought how posh she had become, with her tidily combed hair and velvet cape.

Elise growls at Marie. She is thinking on the unfairness of it – that she is stuck with a grown up daughter who is still a child in her head; no good for anything but playing doll's houses all day.

'There be nothing wrong with you, how 'bout making some hot soup for your mother?' Berthe instructs.

Marie wanders over to the stove. It is true that her mother has tried to teach her how to cook but she forgets in which order to do things. Soup – well that wasn't too difficult, she thinks to herself. Just peel and chop the suede and turnips and pop them in a pan of boiling water. Oh – and salt – and pepper, but how much? Marie frowns; she can't remember how much salt so she puts in a handful. That should do it, she reckons.

'Your mother's had her medicine,' Berthe slurps, finishing off the dregs in the bottom of a pewter mug. 'You be sure she has some of that soup and I be back in the morning.'

Marie is used to being left on her own, but not necessarily in charge. Sometimes she was left with her baby and sternly told she was 'in charge'. It was all right when the baby didn't cry, when she was all soft and warm and nestled close to Marie's breast. But when Catherine cried it was frightening, Marie couldn't get her to stop. The baby would lie in its crib, kicking its legs and flaying its little arms about. That was when Berthe told her about the medicine – her special medicine, and it worked. Berthe would make some up before Elise and she went out for their 'relaxation'.

'Ah … relaxation,' Berthe slowly enunciated, sniggering.

Marie wanted to go as well.

'Not on my life!' Elise jibed, 'you be a mother now. Your place be at home.'

It was nice for a while, when the baby had grown a little. She sat on Marie's knee, laughing and clapping her hands. Then, when she could crawl and walk, they played games together, hide-and-seek and catch-and-throw. But the baby grew bigger still and began to put words together and soon Catherine had more words than her mother and could put them together faster.

Next, the toddler began to take notice of her grandmother, climbing up on the wooden chair by the stove where she could watch Elise Dupont cooking. It wasn't long before Catherine was rolling out pastry and even cutting up vegetables. Marie feels upset, thinking about this; it is a strange mixture of jealousy and longing. Catherine would have known what to do with the soup. Marie wanders over to the soup pan and adds a handful of pepper for good measure. She is daydreaming about Chevreul, about his talk of schooling. He had spoilt everything – soon little Catherine was counting numbers and writing her name. Writing her name! 'Catherine', her baby had written in perfectly formed letters, and Marie realised that her baby wasn't a baby anymore, but a little person who was cleverer than she was and yet still threw a tantrum at the slightest thing.

'The soup be ready,' Marie tells her mother, a hint of pride in her voice.

Elise Dupont attempts to pull herself up on grimy pillows. She is clammy; her greasy hair lays matted against her head.

'I squashed the vegetables through a piece of muslin,' Marie beams, plonking the bowl and a piece of bread on her mother's lap.

'I can't reach the spoon. Help me child.'

Marie fills the spoon and places the object between her mother's lips. Elise sucks hard, slurping the hot liquid into her mouth.

'What the hell!' she cries, as the liquid is spat out, dribbling down her chin and splattering onto the crumpled bedcover.

'Mercy me, how much pepper you put in this soup? It be choking me!'

Marie's bottom lip trembles. 'I tries to do it proper ... I tries!' she cries, running from the room, in embarrassment and fear.

Death

A damp mist hangs in the air over Paris. Berthe Rouart struggles through the swirling haze, her head covered by a tattered shawl. She would make a good subject for one of Seurat's charcoal sketches, but over a year has passed since the women rolled home after the café-concert, and now Seurat is far removed from the world of painting. He lies in a delirium. He doesn't know in which bed he lies, in which house, but even in his feverish state his mind mentally seeks out his studio, his private quarters.

Here he would have a sense of familiarity. Here his spirit is pulled towards his secret life. It is only fitting that the image of his mistress Madeleine floats ghost-like in his mind, for had he not made her into a ghost, a mere spectre of the flesh and blood relationship that they enjoyed? He had immortalised her forever in his portrait, *Young woman powdering herself.*

He felt ambivalent towards the painting because it betrayed an attachment to the materiality of flesh, something he had attempted to transcend. He had failed to suppress her voluptuousness, to bind it with the rigours of his artistic asceticism. He had even put himself in the painting; his image captured by a small self-portrait which had been strategically placed – hung on the wall of Madeleine's dressing room. Within the painting Seurat's gaze fixes upon his lover as she powders her face. He would have been immortalised, in the role of a voyeuristic onlooker, if a friend had not advised him that the self-portrait looked ridiculous. Seurat could not bear the ridicule and heeded his friend's advice. The self-portrait was painted over and replaced by an innocent object; a vase of flowers.

But Madeleine could not be reduced to an object – a thing – a mere architectonic form. She was flesh and blood; far more to Seurat than the calculated, painterly representation of human desire – and the warm, living, moving body of his child had come from her flesh.

It is all images floating in a mist. Seurat momentarily opens his eyes and thinks he sees his son, an engaging toddler, hovering at the side of the bed. Seurat groans, claws at his throat. His larynx is closing; no air can pass through this burning area of pain. He wants to hold the child close to him but the image dissolves like molten rock. Ah – they had broken free of form; his lover and their child had become liquid and he was dissolving too, burning up with fever. Soon they would be nothing but a river of hot lava.

Berthe hurries along; she is looking forward to the warmth of the Dupont's stove but senses something is amiss as she pushes open the wooden door. A dank coldness hits her, and the fetid smell of leftover soup and sweat fills her nostrils. She pulls the tattered shawl from her head and lifts the corner of a woollen hat. The sound of talking, interspersed with sobbing, draws her attention to the corner of the room. Marië is huddled on the floor, next to the doll's house.

'There, there, little baby, don't you be crying – the doctor be coming soon.'

Marie reaches into the doll's house and rocks a miniature crib with the tip of her finger, whilst letting out a muted cry.

Berthe experiences a watery, nauseous sensation in the pit of her stomach. She crouches down by Marie and places her hand under the young woman's chin, with a gentleness out of keeping with her usual bombastic gesturing.

'It be cold in here child, what 'bout keeping your mother warm?'

Marie stares with tormented eyes, tormented but angry because of her inherent insolent look. The gaze is fixed on the opposite corner of the room, on her mother's bed.

'I killed her ... it be all my fault ... it be the soup that did it!'

Seurat is aware of a presence in the room, of the trickle of water and a hand stroking a cool cloth across his forehead. His eyes are shut; the hand could belong to his mother or his mistress but he is past the point of deciphering who is seeing to his needs.

His mind is far removed from the reality of his present situation, though he'd experienced a strong sense of foreboding the previous few weeks. He had been thinking about death, impossible not to having recently hung the paintings of his friend Dubois-Pillet, who had died of smallpox the year before. The paintings hung alongside his own for the Salon des Indépendants. Seurat worked hard hanging the paintings, not feeling quite himself because his throat hurt. The illness had persisted for a number of weeks and in his feverish state he thought he could see the microscopic spores that floated in the Paris air. The spores had the appearance of tiny coloured baubles, suspended in space, transforming the Paris skyline into a landscape composed of luminous dots. One of the baubles was surely lodged in his throat? The doctor informed him that he was suffering from an infectious quinsy and needed to rest in bed. Seurat felt unable to rest whilst the paintings needed hanging and he worked himself into a stupor.

Seurat feels the trickle of water across his face. In his fevered mind he is lying by a cool mountain stream that lulls him with a gentle rippling sound. Suddenly, in the background, he hears the pounding of a horse's hooves. The pounding of hooves draws closer. Seurat is confused. How has this creature escaped the confines of his painting, the last painting he had hung – his unfinished work, *The Circus*? The creature's heavy breath is upon his face; its nostrils flaring in the dimly lit candlelight. Seurat struggles to open his eyes. Where is the pretty bareback rider, surely she must be here too? He cries out, a strangulated cry that forces its way through his constricted throat. The room is full of torsos, they walk towards him, they disappear through the walls in the room – they pass through his body. There is no containing the images as he had once done through his numerous studies of classical statuary. The fragmented body parts have broken free of their smooth plaster casts; they shake their truncated limbs before him.

Berthe Rouart has never seen a piece of classical statuary but she knows, as she looks upon the body of Elise Dupont, that something transforms human flesh at the point of death. Despite the dirt and grime her friend looks peaceful, the years of care and self-abuse strangely cleansed from her face.

Berthe does not panic in the face of death, it is a common enough occurrence, and a sense of inevitability quickly covers grief.

'Come child, we need to see 'bout having the body taken away – it be crawling with disease and that spread quickly.'

Marie lets out a long, plaintive wail and rocks the doll's cradle faster still. 'It be all my fault! The soup – I made a mess of the soup. The doctor be coming soon ... he be coming soon!'

Grange Farm

Nov 23 – 1981

Dear Tony,

I am saddened to hear about your illness – it must be a terrible shock for you and your family. It feels hard to take in as you looked so well at Sophia's twelfth birthday party. We will, as ever, stay in close touch over this – I want to support you as much as I can.

Tony you mentioned that you wished you had my faith – but that the starkness of your situation is not enough to kick start you into religious territory. I know that you say this with your usual sense of humour and I am not about to begin to try and dissuade you from a position that you have firmly held all your adult life.

But if you can bear with me I would like to share something with you that I have only ever shared with Mannie. It is the story of how I lost and then re-found my faith. I'm not certain of my motives in re-telling this now so please forgive my presumption – I just feel I'd like to share this memory with you.

In my early twenties there was so much circumstantial pressure to make me question my faith: the events of the war, the cruelty and sadism on a mass scale, and at a more cerebral level the eloquent arguments of Einstein (who was a truly benevolent man who argued for the sanctity of human reason and the ability and will of humankind to work in unison for the common good). Good and evil were pitted against each other in non-religious terms – though Einstein did not forgo the notion of 'spirit'.

You and I once discussed this at length if you remember?

However, it was not the global impact of events, or the thoughts of a great mind, that sent me tumbling into a dark space of doubt concerning the veracity of a personal God. It was, in fact, the death of my childhood mentor, Agnes Phipps, and the way in which she died, that toppled me into disbelief.

The last time I saw Agnes was in 1944 – just prior to starting my undergraduate studies. My mother and I met her for tea, at her home, that had always been close to the village school where she taught. She was a sweet, slightly eccentric woman – a spinster who had lost a loved one in the First World War and as with so many women of her class made her way in the world as a school teacher.

Agnes was enjoying retirement – taking time to pursue her interests; she was very knowledgeable about botany. She wanted to travel a little, to extend her collection of pressed wild flowers, all of which she had sketched and painted, most skilfully, as a record.

We exchanged a couple of letters the first term of university as I had always kept in touch with her – but there followed a gap in communication. I did not think on this – being caught up in the excitement of my new life. One day I received a letter from my mother informing me that Agnes had been murdered. It was pitifully tragic. She had been out for the day – collecting wild flowers in an isolated spot – and was found dying from stab wounds. The police could glean no apparent motive, concluding that it was a senseless murder.

The world had been overrun with violence during the

war but this assault on my personal memory of a dear person went deep. All of the usual questions hit me again – forcefully.

Why did evil happen with alarming regularity? Why was prayer no protection against evil? Was prayer a protection against anything at all? Why did life negate the Sermon on the Mount? If God cared about 'the lilies of the field' and 'birds of the air' where was his care for us? On and on it went. How, I asked myself, could I have been so deluded?

I tried to meditate on Christ's gospel of forgiveness but it was of no use – I found I couldn't possibly forgive the person(s) involved in Agnes's death. For months I was in a mental fog and purposively shut all thoughts of God out of my mind. I removed religious ritual from my daily life, throwing away my rosary beads – a precious gift to me as a child from my mother. And whenever I though of Agnes I was consumed with a burning anger.

Mine was a humble epiphany. I was at home for the weekend putting together some belongings, as I was moving into a larger room at my college lodgings. It was a few weeks before you and I met. I'm sure you thought I always came across as confident regarding my belief in a personal God. I did not share with you the degree of uncertainty I had recently experienced.

Anyway – there were many reminders of Agnes whilst sorting through my belongings. I found old school books, essays she had marked, and of course my first telescope, which Agnes had chosen as a school prize. Her voice came back to me so clear – as though she were literally speaking inside my head.

'Ralph, with this telescope you will explore wonders and no doubt it will set you on the path to many discoveries. Do not forget that it is God, in his wisdom, who has given us minds that are capable of thinking and questioning. Do not expect to find all of the answers. To allow a life where we know all of the answers would be a folly on God's part; can you imagine how boring it would be to know everything – to be drained of wonderment?'

Then she smiled, gave a little laugh and continued. 'Build your faith on doubt – doubt does not destroy, it strengthens.'

Did Agnes really say this to me as I proudly walked up the aisle during the school assembly to collect my prize? I can't clearly remember, but it seems rather too many words for her because she never took up space; she liked to give that to others.

After sorting the rest of my things I went to the local church – the one I had always attended with my mother. I sat at the back and surveyed the familiar scene; the huge crucifix suspended from the roof – from which, as a child, I had imagined Christ flying, as if he were some superhero. And then the statue of Mary – her gaze of beatific love fixed on me. Lastly, the baptismal font – the spot where my mother had handed me over to this world of faith and ritual.

'I doubt you God,' I spoke in a whisper that did not lack vehemence. 'I doubt you in every fibre of my body and every brain cell that fuels my mind.'

But the words were not thrown out into a void – they were absorbed by a presence that wrapped itself around me and held me while I cried. This presence has remained with

161

me, it has never deserted me, and I choose to call it God.

So when I say, 'God be with you,' this is what I really mean Tony – and I will go on praying that it might be so.

Your friend always, Ralph

PS Apologies – but if it is OK with you I am lighting a prayer candle each time I go to mass.

Claremont Hospice

Jan 2 – 1982

Dear Ralph,

Forgive me for not replying to your letter sooner – I know you understand my situation.

First, let me stress Ralph that if anyone is to say a prayer for this lost atheist soul let it be you – there is no need for you to 'apologize' and strangely it has given me comfort to know that you are lighting prayer candles.

Now I understand that my refusing medical intervention might seem like an act of suicide and that I must be a proverbial pain in the arse to the medics, who are intent on prolonging life and do not want to be seen to be condoning euthanasia by proxy; but the reality of my situation goes beyond academic debate.

What is happening to me is for real!

Ralph – I am so weary of this illness – but what I really want to share with you is that somehow, from within this weariness, I have touched upon a sense of inner peace.

I hardly deserve to experience this, having rejected all forms of religious belief, and of course I could continue down my sceptical path to question whether my experience is due to some endorphin fuelled trip courtesy of the brain, in its evolutionary quest to ease us through the transition from life to death.

I am not saying that I have discovered God Ralph – just that I understand more of what you tried to describe to me. So my friend, I rely on you to continue to pray, but only for a quick release – because the cancer is too

163

advanced for the situation to improve.

And rest assured Ralph – if there is 'something' the other side defying what we know from physics – I'll be there to meet you and I will have to apologize to the Catholic Magisterium (and to you) for my rants against their 'meddling'.

Your affectionate adversary,

Tony

The Right Time

Mannie gathers up the dishes, having decided that meal times are an anomaly on Ward B, considering none of the patients seem able to eat. The heat is adding to her sense of claustrophobia and she walks over to the open doors. She wishes the doors were a porthole to a parallel world of freedom. In this parallel world Ralph is healthy and together they can do whatever they desire.

Mannie thinks of all the interesting places they might have visited if things had gone according to plan. Recently there had been a television programme on couples who dared to sell up, having decided to live out their twilight years in the Nevada desert. You could go it alone or live on an organised site.

'We'd probably have gone it alone, wouldn't we? We were never that sociable, as a couple,' she confessed to Ralph and he had stared at her, uncomprehending of this admission of her dream.

'We'd have lived really simply and watched the sun go down every evening, a special kind of privacy and isolation ... bliss.'

All these years later, Mannie still can't quite let go of the notion that she should be planning an exciting itinerary for their Winnebago adventure – not writing a diary about death.

When does a human being know they are ready to die? I feel you reached that place of knowing long before you went into hospital and now I feel guilty. Should I have helped you to seize the moment Ralph – should we have seized it together?

We used to talk about death before you got sick, how it would be hard for one of us to be left without the other. I expect all couples talk like this – or maybe they don't talk at all – too afraid to think about these things. Perhaps some leave it until death seems more tangible.

But we did talk and I know that you were afraid, not so much of death but of an undignified death, of all the things that are happening to you now. Because everything does happen to you; you have no will, no power to stop this horrible decline, to prevent your body and mind from torturing you.

When was the moment Ralph?

When you smashed some of your equipment in the attic out of frustration because you couldn't remember the sequence of using it anymore? Or something more banal, a pan of boiling water spilt perilously near to the cat – burning your foot as it crashed to the floor? Or the moment your bladder and bowel wouldn't function and I had to coax you to the loo like a small child – or the moment when it all became involuntary, urine and excrement everywhere?

Perhaps it was when you hit me for trying to encourage you to undress and immediately betrayed such pain and angry disbelief in your eyes? Or the moment Sophia came to visit with Kerry and you looked at your beloved daughter and grandchild totally mystified as to who they were?

We never used to sit down for breakfast; we wandered about the farmhouse kitchen via well-worn tracks. We passed each other with morning papers and magazines, you with your buttered toast and cup of tea, me with something warm from the Aga. It all felt happy, familiar. I wouldn't see you for hours, my day was my own and I never minded this; knowing that later we would meet and chat and you'd probably tell me about something that had excited you.

It all seems like a dream to me now Ralph. Was our life a dream and is this thing that took over, that has dominated the past ten years, our true reality? Did I wake from some lazy, plentiful sleep one morning to the pinching of real life – brutal and hard? When was the protective spell cast – during our holiday on the moors all those years ago? Oh why couldn't it have lasted, lasted forever?

There was a day when I forced you to sit at the kitchen table, a napkin round your neck. I spooned in your breakfast – the bread was crumpled, the jam dropped, the tea was slurped. Was this the moment Ralph? You looked at me with such disdain.

'I don't like this' you hissed at me.

'I don't either,' I replied, and it seemed as though these were the only words we could draw from almost forty years of marriage. But you see we had agreed on this as on most things. Our joint despair was a marker of some underlying certainty.

Should we have acted on that despair? I can understand how people do. But the moment passed and our independence with it. Others took over and now it is others who keep you alive and I can only look on and wonder, wonder – what is the point of all their medical heroics ?

Daydreams

Sophia returns to bed – more relaxed now. She dozes and daydreams about the new baby. She doesn't want to know the sex of the child in advance because she likes to replay the delicious sensation in her mind of being told, 'It's a boy!' or 'It's a girl!'

Her father had been five years into the illness when Kerry was born. God how he had aged; the dementia had ravaged his good looks as well as his fine mind. She placed a wriggling Kerry in his arms and he looked startled, almost afraid, as though he wasn't sure what a baby was. Perhaps he thought the baby was a part of himself, that he had spawned this little body out of his own weakened flesh.

Mark was put off by the idea of this, but he was only too aware that his wife always did go in for skewed notions. Sophia felt strangely comforted by the idea that her father might think that the baby was a part of himself – and anyway, it was sort of true.

The thought of the new baby energises Sophia – at least enough to enable her to get up and prepare tea. She sings a little whilst debating what to make that will be quick and easy. Sophia has been told that she inherited her singing voice from Camille but she doesn't remember being cradled in the arms of her grandmother. She was, after all, only an infant when her grandmother died.

'I don't like opera,' she informed Mark, soon after they'd met, as they swapped family histories. ' And I'm sure my grandmother wouldn't have been able to identify with contemporary music.'

Sophia belts her songs out; from the punk movement onwards she has identified with the strong woman trying to break into a male orientated music world. Her great grandmother, Catherine Dupont, never considered the politics of what she did. She loved to sing, to feel the power of her allure for men. In some ways she was freer than Sophia because she didn't worry about sexual politics; there was no room for this on the Parisian stage. She was there to draw attention and this was what gave her pleasure. No point in having admirers and not enjoying what they had to give, such as presents, money and eventually a kept existence by some elderly 'client'.

The child? The child had been a mistake, the result of her initial innocence, but Catherine learnt to look after herself, to protect herself. There was no place for innocence in the world she inhabited, a half-lit world of surface glamour where women existed purely as a symbol for male desire. There would be no more babies, but sometimes she made her way to her guardian's residence and watched for her daughter. She might catch a glimpse of her and then she thought how sensible the child appeared, not spirited as she imagined the rest of the Duponts to be.

Within this moment Catherine felt lost, for she had no real knowledge of her natural mother, Marie Dupont. She had fragments but couldn't be sure these were real memories. One of these fragments was the memory of a doll's house, situated in a rather sparse room. Very sparse, she thought to herself as she pondered on her collection of trophies. Then she remembered three shadowy figures. One of the figures was a young woman called Mama. The young woman would sometimes kiss her, despite looking cross much of the time. Catherine also remembered two larger women who were exuberant and noisy, but not really ill natured. Monsieur Berri had taken her away and she only visited the women a couple of times. One day her guardian told her that her grandmother had died and that her Mama had disappeared. She never did learn what had happened to her mother. But above the well meaning, considered input of the Berri household she remembered a sense of 'something' that she couldn't put a word to. Later she decided that the word 'feisty' might do. There was something feisty in her blood and it had determined her life.

Sophia might have approved of Catherine, even if she couldn't fit her into her feminist scheme of things. She recoils from being compared with Camille; Camille who symbolised a sorry life, a life of being bullied by an irate husband.

The story of Netta, her maternal grandmother, is much preferred, especially as she had lived long enough to figure as a real person in her granddaughter's life. Sophia had witnessed her grandparents' relationship and she knew that being in their presence had always induced in her a sense of ease. Her grandfather was a mild mannered man who treated his wife with affection and respect. But there was courage beneath her grandfather's mild ways – he had been quite a hero in the Second World War Netta assured her – and Sophia decided from a very young age that she rated this kind of masculinity.

'Strength and softness,' she explained to Mark, who teased her about her categorisations of people.

'So, what about me?'

'Well – my mother married someone similar in character to her father; I suppose I've done the same. Not in the academic sphere though!' she added laughing.

Mark smiled at this. It was true that he found Ralph's intellect a bit intense but he recognised that his father-in-law was a warm and kindly man and it was a compliment to be compared favourably.

'I think your parents took some time to get used to me though – probably thought I was going to spend my whole life strumming a guitar.'

'Strumming a guitar … what's strumming?' Kerry asked.

'Like this,' Mark mimed.

Sophia felt a rush of anger thinking back to the time when she and Mark had been in a band. It was all they wanted to do for a while and Mark would have gone on playing full time if he could; but life and family commitments had caught up with them and they both ended up in regular jobs. Sophia still performed in a local band at the odd charity gig and wrote lyrics, which she often furtively hid away. For all of her outward bravado she still struggled to rate her creative abilities.

A lingering resentment persisted concerning this period of time. It wasn't as though her mother was truly old fashioned; she was in fact a free spirit in her own way. But there was something naive, otherworldly about Mannie that niggled. Sophia felt her mother didn't understand the political nature of life and that her never having to fight for anything had made her colourless.

Sophia feels guilty about these negative thoughts. After all she'd pretty much had her own way – like when she'd decided to go backpacking in Australia instead of going to college. Her parents had funded the trip and then she'd met Mark and decided to get married. Mark was incredulous when he first met Sophia. 'Booted straight into work, that was me,' he told her. 'What a spoilt girl you are.'

Perhaps she was spoilt, spoilt enough to sometimes resent the settled suburbia life she now enjoys. But none of this matters on a hot summer's afternoon as she croons to her unborn child and thinks about her father; how he will never understand about this grandchild. The song that she sings is melancholy, out of character, but this is because Sophia doesn't consciously know about the birdsong and the way in which it connects everything.

Seurat's Boat

Seurat has less than twenty-four hours to live, but he clings to life as though conscious that this abrupt closure is far too soon. There are not enough paintings to lay down for posterity. His fevered brain recognises the fact. He has only made a beginning and there is so much more that he needs to express.

There is a commotion in the room; a fluttering that brings the image of white doves into Seurat's mind. Their feathers are of the purest white and the outstretched wings brush softly against his cheek as the birds calm and settle upon the bed. He wants to paint the snowy creatures, to portray the gentle flapping with a thousand sparkly dots. From afar a voice is calling, 'Not my child, not my baby too,' but he cannot grasp that the voice is Madeleine's and he is unaware that his son is also ill.

Ralph would say that Seurat is fortunate because the doves are the kindest of birds, and if the doves come for a person they are assured a place in heaven. Ralph knows that the doves haven't come for him yet and this confuses him. He cannot figure whether he has died and heaven has eluded him or whether death has eluded him and he is in some strange waiting room. He senses the latter.

The seascape is uninteresting except when a sailing boat

arrives. Ralph has been aware of the sailing boat for some time and has struggled to put together a sequence of events. The sea splashes against the huge rock, calmly or ferociously, depending on the wind's direction. Ralph watches with a transfixed stare; he is uncertain as to whether he arrived at the island on this vessel, or by other means, but then he remembers the flock of messenger birds; how they had grabbed him in their beaks and roughly deposited him on the rocky shore.

There *is* a sequence of events. The top of the huge rock opens and the doves fly free, scattering the steel-grey messenger birds that dominate the sky. The sailing boat can be seen bobbing on the horizon. It could be minutes, it could be days, but he is certain that the two events are connected. Ralph's mind has struggled; it has fizzed and pushed the contours of his brain as a thought desperately tries to form. Ralph has tried to formulate a thought about endings and he reckons he has succeeded. His excitement is immense. The thought bubbles over as he shakes his head and shouts excitedly.

The arrival of a boat signals an ending and a beginning. But it is the ending that Ralph seizes upon. When the doves are released a sailing vessel arrives; hence a human being must have died. Once the boat is anchored by the shoreline there is a chattering in the wind, a sense of anticipation. Ralph wonders if God holds a big party in the cave, a welcoming ceremony for the souls that have slipped ashore. And his eyes become moist with angry tears because a part of him is instinctively conscious that he is still forced to walk the island, to huddle in its nooks and crannies seeking safety. He is acutely aware that his time hasn't come.

But Seurat's time is close. Madeleine Knobleck is paralysed with fear. Her lover is dying and her child is sick. She is caught up in the immediacy of the terror of losing all she holds dear. She watches as Seurat claws at thin air, crying out words she doesn't recognise. He is both mesmerised and afraid of the doves; fearing he will choke on the dense mass of white feathers that brush up close to his face. The feathers become a billowing white canopy that is flung over his entire body. He watches the canopy slowly descend, an unfurled roll of silk that never quite covers him. As he looks up he can see patches of sky, blue and white, tinged with pink. Then he realises that he is peering at the white sails of a sailing boat against the horizon. He scrutinizes, with the studied attention of an artist's eye, but feels compelled to do nothing other than lie back and relax. This is the most beautiful sky he has ever seen but it is the one he will never paint.

Stories

Sophia realises her father's death is imminent. His disinterest in food and agitation when it is forced upon him upsets her. She has nightmares about this cruel ending, afraid that it may involve a slow process of dehydration. In recent weeks she has spent entire visits trying to encourage Ralph to take a sip of tea and a teaspoon of mashed solids. Strangely, since the hopelessness of the situation has hit her, many of her memories revolve around food. She remembers family picnics in the garden; long sprawling summers filled with carefree play.

It is true that her father was often lost in some project but she can still capture his comforting presence, as he waved from the attic-viewing platform, like a prince locked in a high tower. The memory of this makes Sophia smile. She had imagined herself as a princess running free and her father as a hero waiting to be rescued. This was a strange reversal of all the fairy stories she had been told as a little girl. Sophia stays with this thought for a while. She sees herself in green gingham, her school dress, a petulant child arguing with Mannie.

Sophia feels a pain in her chest. The more she holds onto the memory the worse the pain becomes. What had they been arguing about? Who was to take tea and biscuits to her father? Yes – that was it! So – she had been jealous of her mother? Sophia is stunned by this recognition. Had Mannie, in turn, been jealous of her? Possibly, but it was more likely that she had been protecting Ralph's working space. Sophia suddenly sees the situation from the other side. It must have been difficult for her mother trying to coax a demanding child to understand that her father was working and that he didn't want his concentration broken. Her mother had tried to be part of her playful world but Sophia now realises the extent to which she had shut her out, making her a witch-like figure in her childhood fantasies – a witch who imprisoned Sophia's beloved father in a high tower, forbidding little princesses to come near.

Sophia thinks she remembers a day when the indifference to her mother set in. She had been playing near to Mannie in the garden; waiting for a friend of her father's to arrive with his two sons. Her mother had been happy that day; she had sat close by – content to watch Sophia make mud cakes for when the boys arrived.

'Mind you don't get too mucked up,' Mannie had chuckled, for it was not really a reprimand.

The mud cakes were spooned onto little red plates. Sophia recollects that this had been done with some precision, as she was careful not to splatter the fine gold line that had been delicately painted round the edge of the plates. The tea set had been a favourite plaything. The tiny cups and saucers required careful handling as they were made of china. She recalled her grandmother saying that plastic might have been better. But Sophia loved the tea set with its hand-painted milk jug and matching teapot. She waited in readiness while her mother chatted away, and every now and then she would gaze up at the attic window, knowing that her father would come down once the visitors arrived.

The boys arrived, rushing past the mud picnic. They were each carrying a metal biscuit tin. At first Sophia thought they had brought real biscuits in preference to her offerings, but when the tins were emptied out a pile of brightly coloured plastic bricks fell onto the grass.

'Lego!' the boys chanted in delight and began to fit the pieces together to form a number of shapes.

'Brm ... brm ...' one of the boys shouted as he attached some rubber wheels to his invention.

Sophia jumped excitedly, with the realisation that her child's heart had found a way into her father's world. She learnt to copy the boys; an acknowledgement that tea sets weren't of much interest to daddies who were scientists. She copied, and she learnt how to surpass her little friends with her inventiveness – feeling rewarded when her father's eyes lit up with pleasure, 'See how clever she is!' he murmured in delight.

This was the time she felt her mother draw away from her, becoming distant, almost brooding. Had Mannie drawn away or had she pushed her? Sophia decides she had pushed her. All of her 'little inventions' had been for her father and she had purposively hidden them away from Mannie.

'No mummy, Skipper says it's a secret!' she remembers saying, and if her mother tried to intrude the Lego was thrown across the floor in a tantrum.

Her parents rarely argued but Sophia recalls a turning point – the beginning of some tension creeping into the house. There were tears behind closed doors and her father's calm voice, always calm, but with an edge to it. Netta had been her comfort during these tense years.

'Your mother wants something too much,' Netta had told her.

Sophia recollects being about twelve at the time.

'What does she want so much?' she probed, a little uncomfortable at this declaration of her mother's greed.

'Something that won't happen now, the time's gone past and besides it's a family curse.'

Sophia thinks of her grandmother's careless words and feels tears welling up again. Netta had meant no harm, her comments were the foolish talk of a woman of a particular generation, but the impact of those words had tied a chain of hostility around her heart and made her resent her mother. Now she is afraid, fearful of the fact that her childhood memories are given over to her father. She has made him the guardian of everything there is to tell; all of the stories of her childhood's imagination are bound up with Ralph. Mannie has become a mere onlooker – banished to the periphery. She sees her now, an anxious face peering through a window that is frosted over with antipathy. Sophia raises her hand to stroke her mother's face and bursts into tears.

Thomas's Education

Camille was frequently in tears, not for herself but for her child. Ralph had been a sickly baby; it was as though the effort of surviving nine months in the womb had taken all of his strength. But at least he had survived; the tiny, squirming bundle that was placed in her arms triggered a strong protective instinct.

The baby loved to be sung to. Perhaps this was what first instigated the wrath of Thomas Drew. His wife had always sung to him; to placate him, to soothe him, to woo him. Was the baby going to take his place in her affections? As the months went by he could feel no pride in the child, albeit a boy. It was a fragile little thing and as the years passed the situation didn't improve. Ralph was given to clinging to his mother, showing no inclination towards the usual boyish activities. Despite Thomas's protestations he preferred to stay at home, close to Camille, showing an eager interest in reading books and talking to his mother.

Thomas listened to the pair, whilst pretending to be wholly absorbed in some practical task. He would never admit it – that the sound of his wife's gentle voice calmed him – and he was getting an education into the bargain. Camille touched upon subjects that he had no awareness of from his sparse education. School had been a place of terror, where he was beaten for the slightest misdemeanour, where his curiosity had closed up and sealed off from the bullying presence of his teacher.

Now he listened to stories, Greek fables, bits of poetry; all read in Camille's patient, clear voice. He sat by the firelight and listened but never showed any appreciation.

'The boy should be outside – playing with the others!' he grumbled.

Camille simply stared at him, an open stare that expressed neither anger nor acceptance. She knew the feelings of jealousy were too complicated for her husband to unravel. Later she would stroke his forehead, kissing it softly in the middle, where a strange, burning pain had settled.

Here lay a tightrope for Camille to walk across. She was fearful of Thomas's fiery temper lashing out at the boy. Ralph had become the object of the untrammelled love she desired from her husband, and her assertiveness was pitched at protecting her son. Plates were sent flying when Ralph refused to eat, a constant problem due to his weak digestion and Thomas had once kicked the child for wetting himself. The worst incident was when he held Ralph under water whilst trying to wash his hair. This sadistic act broke Camille's resolve not to meet anger with anger, and finding her strength she pounced upon Thomas.

'If you ever touch my boy again I will go back to France! The Berri family will take us in.'

Thomas stood back, unnerved. Camille had never fought back before and he knew that she meant her words. An uneasy truce took place for a while. It might have all been total bleakness had Thomas not been touched by the birdsong. This had created a small pocket of warmth in his brittle heart and on occasions he reached out to Ralph, who was left with a longing for something extra from his father, an addition to the little affection that was given. In later years he decided that this was a harsh dilemma; that it might have been easier to hate his father through and through rather than feel an unexpressed desire for his love.

Now his father shadows him on the island. Ralph cannot figure why his father has not been asked to the party in the cave. He is confused. Does the lack of an invitation mean that Thomas is not really dead, or does it mean that he has died and is skulking around no-man's-land because there's no place else to go? Ralph is afraid of his father's habitat. The trees are blackened and no birds gather to sing. In this place his father is removed from the birdsong and in his own confused way Ralph realises that this is what it means to be in hell.

Passion

Mannie begins to gather her things. This is the moment when she prays for a miracle. If only Ralph would lift his head, look at her and ask her not to go. The indifference distresses her and awakens a yearning that she feels is incongruous for her age. Under the skin she feels like a twenty-year-old.

I was thinking about our second Xmas, December 1959. We'd had a couple of years of 'essential' nesting and treated ourselves to a record player. You bought me Adam Faith's 'What Do You Want?' You weren't really into pop music but you sang along to the record and we danced around the cluttered sitting room in our little flat. I see myself as a child now when I look back. I thought I was mature at the time; wasn't that one of the reasons I'd captured the affections of a man ten years my senior? I was so in awe of you Ralph and even now I can feel that tingling I used to get in my stomach whenever I thought about you holding me.

We had almost stopped making love by the start of the illness. Why did we just accept that? Lots of people start passionate relationships in their fifties and sixties, perhaps more passionate than when they were young. What happened to us Ralph? Was it the years of trying for another baby?

These questions had bothered Ralph too, particularly at the beginning of the illness when he had found himself evaluating his life in rather a startled way. It had been too easy, he told himself, shut away in his own world, to ignore the tension that had grown between Mannie and himself. He saw her in his mind, in all her youthful loveliness. And she had been lovely, totally unaffected – with a natural attractiveness that appealed to him. He had been shy around women, requiring a trustfulness that didn't seem to equate with the confidence of the modern woman. He was inwardly ashamed of this, not being a true chauvinist but simply requiring a 'soft touch', as Netta had once described it. Ralph knew he was nervy, given to moods of depression due to always striving hard to obtain perfection. None of this seemed to faze Mannie, who was gentle, like his mother, and again Ralph felt uneasy about this transparent need in him for mothering.

But he had wanted Mannie to fly. He remembered the time he tried to persuade her to take a degree. He thought about this, pondering on his persistence in the face of Mannie's disinterest. He hadn't planned to ensnare her but in a way he was glad that she had stayed close; he liked being locked in with Mannie.

They unexpectedly found themselves waiting years for a baby. Ralph began to go over this period of time in his mind. How awful it must have been for Mannie – just waiting. Easy for him, he surmised, with his successful career to carry him along. An image of Mannie's face began to haunt him; he could almost trace the lines of disappointment that had grown deeper with the years. Sophia, the birth of their daughter, now she had put a smile on Mannie's face, encouraged the laughter lines, but the other lines took over as the years went on and there were no more babies. His daughter, his deepest treasure, was only an interlude of happiness in his wife's life.

Mixed emotions overtook Ralph and he drew furiously, dozens of lines criss-crossing. He could no longer explain that these were the lines on Mannie's face, the transactions of love and hate, symbolising all of the emotions they had never talked about, never shared.

Talk? All he had done was talk at Mannie, and she had sat at his feet – listening. He had immersed himself in the comfort and familiarity of it all. He was the child again, safe in the comforting presence of his mother and he was also the adult to be revered.

Mannie had needed more than that. He felt this truth, deep in the pit of his stomach where a fluttering and a knotting made him double up. He had held them back as a couple. He had not allowed their sexual love to grow. What had he been afraid of? Perhaps a whole dimension of energy that lay outside and beyond creating a child? They had never quite got there; they had withered within the familiarity and the comfort of what was known and the spark of what might have been lay way back; a young woman, asleep in his arms, while the sun went down over a Northumberland moor. They had taken their part with centuries of lovers, walked centre stage and off again and Ralph couldn't believe how the sentimentality of this thought tore at his emotions and made him weep.

He felt the deceit had simply gone on. The illusion of a child had dominated the middle years of their marriage and he had allowed Mannie to grow old with nothing more than an empty hope to hold onto. The death of her fertility heralded the death of their sex life, or at least the truly sensual aspect of it. There was nothing separate from this wish for another baby between them. Except for one occasion he remembered. Sophia had bought Mannie some perfume; it had a very heady fragrance, not at all what Mannie would usually wear. But Mannie shyly daubed the perfume on and he had responded to this new scent – it was the scent of 'another' woman, another Mannie. If only they had built on that moment, instead of letting it go. Why had they let it go? Because he was too bloody scared, that was why, and his anger grew intense.

Mannie knows none of this, lost in her own troubled thoughts about the past. She gathers up her things, looks at the clock and decides she has a few minutes left before she needs to leave for her bus home.

Identity

Ralph lifts his head in response to Mannie looking at the clock, or perhaps in his perception it is the sudden fluttering of wings, signalling a departure.

'Almost time to go Ralph.'

Time. Ralph is like a rock in a river; time washes over him but it does not alter his position, his sense of being. No – Ralph holds fast. The rest of the mass is carried along by the current, onto the next event, the next little segment of their structured lives – but the structure has fallen away for Ralph, just as he had predicted.

If Ralph could use words he might say that it is only the formality of this structure that has broken down. His mind is attuned to the ticking of the clock; he senses that the object on the wall has significance for the pieces of mass moving around him. When the object reaches a certain appearance the pink mass will start flapping and fretting before disappearing. This is when Ralph feels the pull of the current as it washes over him and tries to grab him in its force. The object on the wall loses its soporific effect and he feels imprisoned within the ticking. If Ralph could reach the object he would smash it to bits. He would destroy time and put an end to it all.

The impulse to smash the object is what Ralph once explained as a moment of clarity. He discovered, as his illness progressed, that there is a strange paradox whereby a confused mind is able to reach an instance of illumination that cannot be accessed by the rational mind.

This was all to do with Ralph's experience of 'loss' or 'lack'. As he veered in and out of rational thought he sometimes had a heightened awareness of his loss of identity. This was a cruel, lacerating perception of loss. At other times he was closer to the sense of having gained a double identity.

The experience of total loss was the most distressing. Ralph had a sensation of physically collapsing in on himself. It was as though his body was dissolving into a tiny black speck that was invisible to the human eye. No one would be able to look at him, touch him. No one would verify his identity by stating, 'Here stands Ralph Drew the eminent scientist and accomplished artist; husband to Mannie, father to Sophia, grandfather to Kerry.'

Ralph had asked himself, at the beginning of the illness, what he needed to retain – what was it that most defined him? Was it his distinguished career or was it his private, very private, personal life? Within this enclosed space Ralph the scientist walked around at ease, spent time with his wife and spent hours dreaming and scheming in his attic room. The external world didn't see any of this did it?

Ralph knew that the external world was receding; that he was destined to shuffle around the periphery of this vast container of human potential. He felt that he was caught between a fear of falling off the edge into an abyss of nothingness and a sense of wanting to fall off the edge. Part of him was drawn to accelerating the process of the inevitable dissolution of his personal identity. But Mannie had him in her net. Mannie needed to keep him in her field of vision and this prolonged the agony.

These were the days when he became angry with Mannie, hostile towards her presence because he blamed her for holding him to his present state. She was a huge, overprotective mother-bird. She squawked, she roughly pecked and heckled him, pestering him into some sense of order. He wanted her to go away.

Yet there were other days when he took comfort from her presence. The squawking was toned down to a gentle cooing and he felt safe within their cosy nest. He sheltered under her warm, feathery wings; sipping tea as though all was well with the world.

Nothing was really normal or well but Ralph mercifully preserved a memory of normality, or at least remnants of something comforting. The remnants were mixed in with emotional pain as everything meaningful had shattered into myriad pieces. Ralph realised that he could never again grasp the whole picture, just little bits. This was enough to remind him that something splendid and gratifying had existed before all this mess.

It was the same when he had odd flashes of genius. The darkness would suddenly light up with intelligent thought, like a firework display going off in his head. Ralph saw the multicoloured stars fly up into the air and he desperately tried to catch them. But the thoughts were extinguished within seconds – and all became dark again.

Ralph can feel himself going further into the dark since his arrival on Blue-Grey Island. It is as though the rocky terrain has very little surface space with which to reflect sunlight. He seems to spend a lot of time crawling through dark caves, which appear to lead nowhere, but there is a sense of direction. Someplace, in the distance, there is a bright light – brighter than any light that Ralph has seen through his telescope. Ralph believes that this light is the face of God.

The Breath of Life

There is a ruined church close to Ralph and Mannie's village. The edifice stands spectral and majestic down a long winding lane that leads to nowhere. If you go to the end of the lane it is like approaching the edge of the earth. There are warning signs and barbed fences urging the curious to go no further. This is the place where Ralph would have chosen to end his life. Here he could have stepped over the boundaries of human protection into a space that is crumbling, disappearing. He envisioned himself slipping over the precipice, diving a long way down into eternity.

Ralph often visited the church, from his paralysed position, in his chair at home. Mannie had strategically placed the chair by the French doors. Ralph visualised the ruin – lingering on the magnificent crumbling stonework; the image filling his mind until the interior of his head became the inner sanctum of the building and his skull bones the architectural remains of a beautiful structure. Here is incredible masonry, finely chiselled, the work of a craftsman. Sunlight pours through the stained glass windows, shimmering down upon the altar.

This is a ruin still filled with energy – it is the ruin of Ralph's mind. Who will peer inside this sacred space? Ralph thought he heard his mother as she pushed against the ancient wooden door, with the deference of one who is used to entering holy places. He remembered her doing this when he was a small child.

They had entered the church together, and Camille had scooped him up in her arms. Ralph recalls the font filled with holy water and Camille splashing the sign of the cross on his forehead before setting him down before a large statue.

'See Ralph, this is the Virgin Mary, Mother and protector of us all, cradling baby Jesus.'

A notion of the sacred had been deeply planted in Ralph's mind and no matter how hard he tugged at its roots they would not come away. He had wrestled with his religious belief at various stages of his life. Creation was so vast – yet Science so plausible. Could there be a God behind the magnificence, a magnificence that was surely being stripped of its mystery? All of the magic was being undone as cause and effect piled upon cause and effect.

Ralph decided that God had given him an enquiring mind and that the process of his enquiry did not necessarily mean that he had to outsmart God. He saw it more as a privilege, to be given access to some of the secrets of the universe. Ralph decided that this access was a mere fragment – a fleeting look at a very small part of all that might be. Humankind would never catch up with God, he reasoned, and there would always be a question left begging when the resources for discovery reached a point of finitude.

'It is the question that enters every child's mind,' he had said to Mannie. 'What was there before there was something? Who or what created the conditions for the big bang? How can something come out of nothing? How can nothing be taken as a starting point for something?'

Ralph decided that despite all of his knowledge he would never be able to answer this question; that no human being could ever find a satisfactory answer. This was the limit of being human – there was this one question that the human mind did not have the faculty for thinking through. Humankind was merely part of the process of a higher power thinking, but it could never be equal to the power, he reasoned. In Ralph's belief system our entire discovery was as easy as the two-times-table to God.

In his dark moments Ralph often returned to the image of the ruined church. The image helped his spirit to remain strong and though he could not express it clearly he felt that his spirit was being re-built outside of his disintegrating body. The more his physical sense of being was challenged the stronger his spirit identity grew. He was aware of Mannie's pain and wished that he could explain this process to her, but the wish was suspended in air – it hung out there – beyond the everyday reality of shaking limbs, of stuttering, stumbling and drooling. He feared that the physical and mental deterioration were all that Mannie could see.

To understand Ralph's experience we must distance ourselves from words, for words are not directly available to him. Ralph knows the difference, at a level of sensation, between the heavy, leaden pull of weak and useless muscles and a spirit body that is so light that it bounces off the earth's surface. His spirit body flies gracefully in the air and Ralph is aware of this and longs for more of this sensation.

Ralph senses that he is chained to the earth, that his spirit can only fly so far. He also senses that the transformation cannot be complete until the last bit of physical existence is dragged from out of him and that this last bit is the breath of life. Ralph longs to stop breathing – he simply longs to be free.

Never Coming Back

It is almost time for Mannie to go. Just within this moment she is reluctant to leave, to return to her empty house.

I am slipping back into my old ways Ralph. Yesterday – as I was doing the drying up, I mixed up the spoons and forks. I reached into the cutlery drawer to sort things and then I realised it doesn't matter anymore; you are no longer here to be confused. I have been clinging onto the imposed sense of order because it makes me feel safe. Like you, I now become fretful if things are out of place. How free we were before Ralph; all of the clutter lay in the external world – but now the clutter is in my mind and any sense of order is placed outside of me. What a strange reversal!

Oh the emptiness in this house now that you are gone. What a huge vacuous space of trivial activity and my mind full of anxiety as to how you are being looked after. Mixing up the forks and spoons – was that an admission that you are never coming home?

When you used to go away to conferences, before Sophia was born, I was frightened here on my own. I lay awake at night, listening to the old timbers creaking and the wind howling as it buffeted the exposed walls. Remembering this I am thinking about my mother, how difficult it must have been for her when my father was away, not knowing whether he would return from the war. But she must have worked hard at keeping hope alive. Hope – I have no hope. I only have certainty, the certainty that you are never coming home.

Sophia asked me if I wanted to sell the house, to move closer to her and Mark. Could I bear to leave the memories, or is the very act of staying here stopping the memories from being anything other than painful. Perhaps if I removed myself from here I could remember in a less painful way?

In my mind I keep returning to the early years of our relationship with such clarity. I wonder – is it time that provides the distance we need to remember clearly? Somehow, it seems safer, easier, thinking a long way back. I seem to remember more of my childhood now than I ever did before – small, comforting moments pop into my mind, like gathering blackberries in late summer with my mother and aunts. The memories are safe, sacrosanct; nothing can happen now to alter my perception of them. The nearer I get to the present the more unstable the memories become – like when I think about the later years of our marriage or recent tensions between Sophia and myself. I feel frightened – it's as though my whole sense of reality could get turned on its head.

Even as I write this I feel anxious for you. Your childhood was far from perfect. Thank God for your mother. I tell myself that Camille must have given you enough happy moments for you to have some sense of peace – some safe haven to return to.

Ralph searches for this peace on Blue-Grey Island. At the

beginning, he found that as he stumbled across craggy rocks or emerged from the darkness of the caves, he would come across a patch of purple heather. He cried out loud with joy as he pulled off his footwear and pushed his feet into the soft, mossy surface. The angel, that has been sent to watch over him, always appeared at this point. Where did she suddenly come from, Ralph puzzled, as the white piece of the mass floated towards him, a billowing cloud of consternation?

'Hush now Ralph – best to keep your slippers on – the ward floor can be tacky.'

The soft carpet of moss had turned to grey – flattened to the surface sheen of slippery rocks that have been repeatedly pounded. Yet there was a trickle of water, a tiny stream.

'Now we will have to change you Ralph, but at least you didn't pee in your slippers. Here – let me fetch them and then we'll go to the bathroom.'

Mannie knew about these 'little accidents' as Ruth kindly put it. She kept hoping that one day she would be told that Ralph had made it to the bathroom on his own, but just now he is confined to bed – too weak to stand unaided. This is foolish, she tells herself, to try and map hope in this way. After all, Ralph has been incontinent for a long time.

I hate it, I hate it! The leakage, the spills – the awful smells. And I feel guilty at my sense of relief that I no longer have the responsibility of feeding you, changing you. I am free to remember you as you were, to run back down the years, to keep a memory burning bright that is denied you.

You are my lovely caring man. Your body is warm

against mine and I am loved and protected by you. I look into your bright, intelligent eyes and see how much love you have to give to me. And I ache inside because I never said any of those words to you and a silence fell upon all that we might have been.

Part Five

Shadowlands

Marie continued to rock the doll's cradle despite Berthe's admonishments.

Berthe sat down to further survey the sorry scene. She was experiencing a strange fluttering in her chest – a fluttering that signified an inward struggle of conscience. This was a new experience for her, never having felt the sharp pinch of duty before. What was she to do with her friend's daughter, a young woman quite incapable of looking after herself?

Berthe struggled some more and then a strange sense of calm settled within her mind. It was as though the mantle of martyrdom had fallen upon her shoulders like a comfortable cloak.

'Well – this be a right to-do, what's to be done with you Marie?'

Marie stared at Berthe with her insolent dark eyes. 'I be coming home with you – can't stay here by myself!'

'No, you can't,' Berthe conceded, as she glanced around the room making a mental note of what she might take.

Elise had collected a fine assortment of cooking ware, not that Berthe was into cooking, but the bowls and pots might come in useful. She would have to persevere with Marie, attempt to teach her how to keep house. It might be a

201

comfort after all to have another body around the place.

'Will you be bringing that doll's house?' Berthe enquired, wondering where it would fit in her cramped living quarters. 'We could make a bit – selling it you know.'

Marie's bottom lip puckered.

'No! The doll's house be mine. Monsieur Berri promised I could keep it.'

Berthe paused for a few seconds. The thought that Monsieur Berri might be of financial assistance had entered her head. She was after all going to be lumbered with another mouth to feed. Ah – but what if he took Marie under his wing, then she would gain nothing because he might take everything. It never occurred to Berthe that Monsieur Berri would have no use for a few cooking pots.

'I will keep this a secret,' she murmured with a great sense of satisfaction. 'He will never find us,' she continued, as the thought of such deception began to escalate into a sense of adventure.

The two women disappeared into the foggy morning air – Berthe bent double with the weight of the cooking pots slung over her shoulder and Marie tottering along with her arms stretched round the doll's house. The mist was devouring bodies dead or alive. A few days later, after the death of her little boy, Seurat's mistress also vanished.

Monsieur Berri never did trace Ralph's great-grandmother, Marie Dupont. When he called at the rooms he found another family installed.

'Gone with the midwife – that's all we know,' a wisp of a woman informed him.

Monsieur Berri felt heavy. He could smell the stench of

202

poverty as he talked to the woman; see the deprivation in the eyes of her children as they clambered round her skirt. He was torn as to what to do. With Marie gone he could protect Catherine from further contact with her squalid background. Was he correct in doing this, he asked himself? He knew that this posed a moral question – was it correct to cut a person off from their blood relatives?

An image of Marie came into his mind. It was through no fault of her own that she was backward, uneducated. But she had traded her own child for a few trifles. What had happened to the money, he wondered? Probably Elise Dupont had spent it all on absinthe; he doubted whether Marie had seen any benefit from it.

On this score Berri was wrong. Berthe had found the money, safely hidden away in one of the cooking pots. She could not believe her luck as she peered inside to see what was clattering. She did not tell her friend's daughter but swiftly pocketed the booty for herself. It was only right, she figured. The money was due to her.

A day of reckoning came for Monsieur Berri, for Catherine was well aware that she had not been born into his family. She had already been told the story of how her mother had traded her for a few coins. Berri had not meant to tell the child but his wife had blurted out the sad facts in an impatient moment.

Catherine had been ten at the time and the outburst did not upset her in the way one would have expected. The knowledge of her background settled quietly to the back of her mind until five years later a strange dream stirred her memory.

She was a child in the dream, a small child, tottering

around a cluttered room that had a cold stone floor. Catherine was acutely aware of the cool stone beneath her feet. She bent down to pick a cake crumb from the floor and as she stood up her eyes met the gaze of a laughing, roly-poly woman.

'It be no good collecting crumbs,' the woman declared, 'come and have a bite of one of these pastries.'

Catherine looked beyond the roly-poly woman to the far corner of the room where she spied another woman, who was younger – thinner, neatly arranging some doll's house furniture in a wooden crate that had been turned on its side. Catherine tottered over and picked up a miniature rocking chair that magically became life sized. She clambered on and began rocking to and fro, faster and faster until the room began to spin.

She woke with her head thumping, and then gradually, as she reached consciousness, an aching emptiness flooded her mind.

'My mother,' she demanded of Monsieur Berri, 'what happened to my mother?'

'She simply disappeared, disappeared into the shadowlands of Paris.'

'Shadowlands' the word captured Catherine's imagination more effectively than any lengthy explanation; it danced around in her mind. She was forever dancing, dancing and singing. It was so dull living with the Berri household, having to have daily contact with her prissy 'brothers' and 'sisters'. They were not unkind to her but she did not fit in. There was something tepid and unadventurous in their ways, in fact they kept saying that she, in comparison, was hot blooded. This heat made her restless, forced her to kick off her shoes and run round the well-kept garden where the Berri children played with decorum. Grinding her feet into the cool grass failed to get rid of the heat.

An image of Shadowlands began to build into a whole location that was as darkly mysterious as its name. Her guardian had unwittingly planted a notion in his young charge's mind, that there existed a place where you could simply disappear if you so desired. Catherine's thoughts became fixed on escape.

One evening, not long after her fifteenth birthday, she was sitting quietly reading, on the stairs. She could not resist eavesdropping as Monsieur Berri entertained friends. The men were discussing the street life of Paris, a conversation evidently not meant for female ears as it was conducted in hushed tones. Catherine crept closer to the door that was slightly ajar.

'You should at least try the opera,' one of the men pressed. 'You spend too much time in your books Berri – what about a little life – a little colour?'

Catherine smiled. Her guardian was not that sort of a man. He was not blessed with elegance and handsome looks like the man who spoke. Berri was plain and earnest and given to good works. Catherine knew about these other kinds of men, from novels that she had read hidden under the bedcovers at night – with the flame from the candle threatening to set the whole bed alight. And she would feel hot herself, even hotter than usual, just thinking about this other kind of man. She decided that she would run away and find one of these establishments where women sang and danced and were worshipped by male admirers. She imagined herself wearing a pretty gown and her hair coiffed in the latest fashion. The image grew in brightness, it beckoned her, and for a moment she stopped quite still – puzzled that such an exciting place might be located in a dreamier, darker space – a space called Shadowlands.

Missing

When Mannie first began to put together the Reminiscence album Ralph was conscious enough of her intentions to feel disturbed by the project. The album was meant to fill in the missing gaps in his mind; the increasing number of gaps that he had to leap across, like jumping a stream by means of stepping stones. He had done that as a lad, out on the moors. He remembered laughing excitedly as he leapt from stone to stone across the bubbling water. And his mother would follow, lifting her skirt to her knees and nimbly making her way to the other side. She was like a gazelle; not that Ralph had ever seen a real gazelle – but it was how he imagined such a creature might move; lightly, gently, gracefully.

His father would be walking in the distance – his face fixed in a stern gaze. It pained Ralph to see the determined gait of his father, marred by his limp; he could not disguise the limp. Later, they sat down together to picnic and his father relaxed a little and asked if they had seen the rabbits scurrying through the gorse bushes.

'I just fancy a nice rabbit pie,' he teased Camille, knowing that she had an affection for the creatures.

Ralph wished there was a photo of this in the album; a normal, happy, smiley family photo. But there had been no photos, no record of his childhood apart from the odd school picture. It was all down to memory. Memory? Ralph could not remember much of his father's side of the family; his grandparents were sketchy figures in his mind. They had been poor, this much he had retained; it seemed the whole family were poor – aunts, uncles, cousins. The vague recollections blurred into one memory; the occasional visit – an exchange of pleasantries or hostilities – depending on how the drink affected his father. His father was not one for 'family'. There was much cursing under his breath about 'did nowt for me' and a 'bloody rough life!'

As for his mother, it was all mysterious, strange. Ralph had wondered once, when he and Mannie were planning a holiday in France, whether to track down the Berri family. But his mother had protested, it was all 'not to bother' and 'we only caused them upset.' 'We' – Ralph wished he'd asked more about this mysterious collective pronoun. He knew nothing of his grandmother, Catherine, other than that she had run away, become pregnant with his mother, and abandoned the baby on her guardian's doorstep to be taken in without any consideration of the consequences. It upset Ralph, the way his mother carried some sense of shame that was not of her own making.

The story of his great-grandmother, Marie, was 'even worse' his mother had informed him. Ralph remembered the conversation. Camille had spoken in heated terms, most unusual for her.

'Your great-grandmother wasn't too bright and gave my mother up to the Berri family for a small sum of money. Can you imagine it – selling your own child? I think the Berris told me about it because they didn't want me to feel that it was my

208

fault I had been abandoned but that there had been something 'unnatural' about my grandmother and mother.'

'What happened to my great-grandmother?'

'Disappeared – without a trace.'

'And your mother?'

'The same. She was on the stage for a while but I don't think Monsieur Berri was inclined to follow her 'career'. Who knows how she ended up?'

Ralph remembered the conversation as the only time his mother had veered towards self-compassion. He had felt sorry for her but disconnected from the story.

It was all so different for Mannie. When they set up home together Mannie brought a box of photographs with her. Here were the landmarks that Ralph lacked: the first steps, the first bike, the first pet, the first holiday.

'My mother wanted to keep a record for my father and I guess the tradition continued once he was home,' she had explained.

Ralph was captivated. He knew in a way that the advent of recording was partly a generational thing. It was unusual to own a camera at the time he was growing up unless one had money to spare. Mannie was ten years younger than he and her parents were wealthy compared to his own. But he suddenly felt bereft; he wanted his own pictures of childhood to put alongside Mannie's.

Visiting Mannie's parents had been like stepping into another world because here was a family who exhibited little tension or strain.

'They did argue sometimes,' Mannie told Ralph, almost apologetic about her trauma free childhood. 'But they always made it up and made it clear to me that they were friends again.'

Of course there had been no money worries for Mannie's parents, Ralph reasoned. They lived in upmarket Cullercoats, in a neat semi that they owned complete with a sea-view. Ralph wished that his mother had a house with a view of the sea instead of a tiny terrace with a dismal backyard. The backyard was not always dismal; in the summer Camille grew geraniums and sweet peas in pots and painted the washhouse door a bright green. Ralph always remembered the flicker of sunlight on the pots and how this came to represent a happy memory for him.

'She painted the handrail as well,' he told Mannie, 'the one by the steps leading down to the yard. I can remember sitting on the steps, shelling peas one summer.'

The memory is gone now but not the feeling; the internal knowledge that even in a very dark world there are moments of tranquillity. It is this sense of security that Ralph searches for on his island. He longs for a glimpse of his mother's face and is driven by a primal certainty that she is close. Ralph has an inner surety that if his father is present then his mother must also be, because despite all the rows, the turmoil, his parents had in their own way been inseparable.

Protection

Mannie also remembers the pots and the brightly painted handrail. She had sat on the steps, leading down from the kitchen door, the first time she met Ralph's mother, whilst she waited with nervous excitement as Camille busied herself in the kitchen.

On arriving she had asked for the bathroom, knowing that the toilet was outside. Ralph had already told her that this was his chosen hiding place as a child, whenever his parents rowed.

Whilst Camille made tea Mannie's eyes scanned the yard. It was an enclosed world, sheltered from the elements by the high walls of the upper terrace. Mannie heard the clatter of children's footsteps on the steep, concrete staircase that laid the other side of the yard wall leading up to the rooms above. Ralph once told Mannie the story of how his mother had insisted that they lived in the lower tenement because she was fearful of his father falling down the stairs. They used his father's war injury as the reason but it was really the drink that was the problem.

Mannie was glad that Ralph's father had been absent on this first visit. Camille carried a tea tray outside, where Ralph had set up a card table and two wooden chairs. Mannie remembers the green baize that covered the table, mottled from years of card and domino playing and how Camille hastily covered it with a hand-embroidered cloth. The chairs were fetched from a brick storehouse built at the side of the toilet. Mannie peeked inside and noted the neat precision with which an array of patio gardening tools were arranged.

When she thinks about it now she feels that Camille's backyard had as much architectural significance as some of the beautiful buildings Ralph and she had viewed on their travels.

She recollects three freshly painted doors; one fronting the toilet, another the storehouse, but it was the third that caught Mannie's attention.

'That leads to the washhouse,' Camille had smiled, as though reading her curiosity.

Then she stood up and walked rather nervously to the door – opening it and gesturing for Mannie to have a look inside. Mannie stared at the old washtub, complete with scrubbing board and mangle. Her mother used a modern machine, where you fed the clothes through and electricity did the rest. Surely Camille didn't still do all the washing by hand?

Camille smiled again. 'It's not so bad,' she explained. 'I can always use my neighbour's machine for the big things and I could have something more up to date if I wanted, but I like to potter out here – at least in the summer months. This is where I have undisturbed time.'

Mannie couldn't understand it; all those wet soggy clothes to be wrung out felt like a form of bondage to her. But as the years went by the image began to crystallize into a different sort of symbol. Now, in her times of deepest upset, she remembers that afternoon with a sense of calm. Ralph, Camille and herself sitting in the sunshine, with the smell of sweet peas wafting in the air. This image was repeated in its various forms over the years.

Occasionally she would help Camille with the washing and it was during these times that they had their best conversations. Camille lost her nervousness when she was physically working and sometimes Mannie arrived in the middle of some domestic project to the sound of singing. Mannie gleaned snippets of information about Ralph's childhood during this shared activity but Camille was careful never to fully betray her husband. Occasionally she would reminisce about her childhood in France and Mannie began to formulate another kind of life for Camille – the life she might have had if she hadn't have met Thomas.

'Your mother needs a bigger space,' she suggested to Ralph, 'her spirit is crushed by the smallness of her surroundings.'

'It's my father's fault,' Ralph complained, he won't let her help on his allotment. She would love to make a garden there.'

Mannie thought about this. She had been to the allotment with Camille on several occasions to collect eggs. It was another clearly defined space. The allotments were more like a series of hedged gardens. Each allotment was accessed through its own wooden gate. Thomas's allotment reminded Mannie of 'The Secret Garden', with its profusion of wild flowers and brambles all mixed in with potatoes, runner beans, cabbages and beetroots. In one corner was a tumble down shed-cum-greenhouse and in another a patched up hen-coop. Mannie sensed that this was 'Thomas's world', and that she and Camille were merely visitors when they went to collect the eggs or vegetables.

On reflection Mannie felt it was better for Camille that her husband had this space; that such was the nature of their relationship that each explosion sent them scurrying to their own private domain. Even now, years later, she felt there was some natural law in all of this and though Sophia would rail against it and accuse her of being old-fashioned Mannie believed she had glimpsed something of value in Camille's way of dealing with a harsh life.

'There is something wrong,' Camille had confided, as they stood holding the four corners of a rinsed sheet.

It was close to the time when Mannie and Ralph were preparing to move and Mannie had stepped up her visits to Camille.

'He brought me speckled hen's eggs and said they were duck eggs – we don't keep ducks.'

Mannie forced back the impulse to laugh as she realised that Camille was truly distressed.

'Yesterday, he couldn't find the keys for the allotment. He got into such a fury and then burst into tears,' Camille continued, crumpling the corners of the sheet between her fingers. 'Just odd little things – you know, makes me feel there's something wrong.'

Mannie began to watch her father-in-law closely on her visits. It meant calling in at different times, relinquishing time on her own with Camille. A slight tremble down one side of Thomas's body became noticeable; she knew he was embarrassed and trying hard to hide the tremor. It reminds him of the limp, she thought, of how he hates to be seen as physically vulnerable.

One afternoon Thomas lost his grasp of a cup of tea she handed him.

'Here, let me help you,' she gently urged as they both bent down to retrieve the cup.

Thomas's eyes locked with hers and Mannie felt paralysed for a second, caught in the crossfire of his startled gaze and her sympathetic response. She read pain and anger in his look and a sense of, 'Don't you dare reveal that you know about this – don't ever respond to my vulnerability.'

Mannie wondered how to tell Ralph. Since their marriage she had acted as a buffer between Ralph and his father. She visited on her own to spare her husband the contact whilst giving his mother companionship. Camille never grumbled, just accepted the excuse that Ralph was busy, but Mannie saw how Camille's face lit up on the occasions he called in. It was always the same; Ralph would walk in and his father shuffled uncomfortably in his chair. He would be sitting, his chest stripped down to his vest top, after washing over the kitchen sink – whilst Camille prepared tea. Mannie thought she would never get used to this show of flesh and she couldn't quite work out why it disturbed her. The two men exchanged few words and Camille usually hovered nervously in the background.

'Have you time for a cup of tea son?' she called from the kitchen.

'No thanks, best to be off, still got lots to do back at home.'

It was always the same.

'This time you have to stay,' Mannie urged Ralph, 'you have to see how bad it's getting.'

Ralph had already seen the deterioration in his father; the loss of weight, the signs of mental confusion, how his boiling anger was toned down to a simpering and whimpering. He wondered at his own lack of involvement; watching his father become a broken man was like watching a stranger, in truth – a stranger might have elicited more of a response.

Despite the niggling sense of guilt regarding his father, there was a more disturbing thought, which Ralph couldn't bring himself to share with Mannie. He never confided that he felt an exaggerated guilt towards his mother – not his father. It had totally unhinged him, watching the reversal of his parent's relationship. This could have been the time for his mother's revenge, but this was not the essence of Thomas and Camille's relationship. The essence was the birdsong, and Ralph watched his parent's relationship transported back to the original site of its being. Here was a reunion, a reinstatement of purpose and belief. Camille was the mother bird once more, tending her baby chick, and the chick responded, opened its mouth to the trickle of bodily sustenance and its heart to the soothing cadence.

At some level Ralph felt sickened. He watched his parents and decided that his birth had shattered the intimacy of their closed union. He was convinced that his mother must have been tormented and oppressed by the impossibility of introducing a third person into a space that was fenced off by his father's jealousy.

Mannie still thinks about the awful time when Ralph's father was forced to go into a home. The deterioration had become severe and, despite his weight loss, Thomas was too heavy for a delicate woman like Camille to lug around.

It was two years after their move to the farmhouse and when Mannie thinks about this event she feels that it was the one time when Ralph's depression almost got the better of him.

You told me that it was what you had sometimes prayed for as a child – that your father would be taken away and then you and your mother would be left in peace. Now he was gone, but time had moved on and your mother was on her own – there was no 'little Ralph' to keep her company or protect her.

I felt heavy Ralph – and I feel guilty admitting this – but I hoped you wouldn't want Camille to come and live with us. I knew that she would never impose on us, but I was afraid of the strength of such a desire in you. You never suggested it and she never asked but I sensed restlessness in you during those years. I think a concern for her was always on your mind and I felt a strange sort of jealousy at this unspoken intimacy between you.

Your father suffered Ralph – there is no doubt on that score. I am constantly reminded now of those awful visits we made, after we had moved. I feel that we breezed in and out unable to cope with the strange intensity between your parents that grew into some impenetrable wall the more ill your father became. I feel even guiltier that I didn't offer Camille greater support. She was such a sweet woman, how could I have set her up in my mind as a rival? I can't explain – it just seemed to happen. Without Thomas in her life I was afraid that the force of her love was bound to come to you as some sort of demand.

I was thinking the other day – its strange isn't it that Sophia was conceived a few months after your father died, like my body needed to make a visible claim over you.

Everything fell into place – you – me – the baby, and Camille in her role as doting grandmother.

She was given such a short time as a grandmother – Sophia taking her first steps will always be connected in my mind with Camille's sudden death a few days later. And what of the preceding years – all the years your mother spent trudging back and forth to that home?

Even to this day I remember her smiling, laughing with pleasure at Sophia's few tottering steps, and my thinking to myself, here is a woman who can take pleasure in another's freedom even though her own life has been fettered, and I thought how much better than me as a person she was and this thought still bothers me.

If Ralph could talk to Mannie he would explain that it was all much more complicated than she had perceived, and that his depression was not due to silently wanting Camille to come and live with them. It was more that all of his childhood fantasies about his mother had been based on a misjudgement of the situation. His mother had not needed his protection though he had needed hers. He could never make up for the loss of his father and once his father had gone there was nothing for his mother to protect him from. The essence of the relationship with his mother had died with his father.

The knowledge of this settled within Ralph's mind like a heavy, jagged piece of rock. It pressed, it hurt, and it jangled his nerves. It was all to do with passion, with the depletion of sexual energy. Protection, protection, protection! He had spent his whole life worrying about protection; how to protect women, how to be protected by them. He wished that he could have given way to dangerous abandon with Mannie. His parent's relationship had somehow hemmed him in and he felt angry at the realisation that in the occasions of their fighting so hard, and then making up, they had entered a zone of passion that Mannie and he had never so much as dipped into.

Awake

None of Ralph's troubled recollections matter now. On Blue-Grey Island memories are like dust motes blowing around, settling where they will. There is no chronology of events. And this is why in the moment of his 'drowning' Ralph can seamlessly move to a sense of his father standing by him, protectively. Sensation moves beyond memory – creates a new fragment in the world of 'might have been', 'should have been'.

Mannie stands up and reaches for her shopping bag. She digs into the bottom and reaches for a bottle of barley water, her mind half-distracted by the thought of a task waiting for her when she gets home. That morning, as she reached for her earplugs, she had knocked the china pot off the bedside cabinet. The pot fell to the floor shattering into several pieces. Mannie was upset, startled by the object's fragility. It had belonged to her mother; it should have been indestructible. She carefully collected the pieces intending to stick the pot back together.

Now, as she is preparing to leave Ralph, a thought begins to niggle. Was her mother trying to tell her something, perhaps pointing out that some things once broken, no matter how precious, could not be mended? Mannie feels the tears welling up.

'I broke Netta's pot today, the one with the little roses,' she tells Ralph, wishing he might understand this one thing.

He perceives a creature – a gentle bird – ruffling its feathers in agitation. He wants to stroke the bird but doesn't know how. There are bits of Ralph that long to reach out but he feels paralysed by a constriction, a painful inertia.

Amy picks up on the agitation. She hugs her cardigan around her and makes a strange little warbling sound. Ralph hears it; it is the trilling of a tiny bird perched high on the cliff face. He is too exhausted to look up – to try and locate the creature. Water is seeping out from the two holes in the space that others call his face and this is draining him.

Ralph is used to this seepage of liquids, as fluids pour from the fissures carved out of the solid mass that constitutes his body. Sometimes this outpouring makes him more comfortable.

Earlier in the day, he had embarked upon a feverish search for his mother. He thought he had caught a glimpse of her as she walked nimbly down the landing platform from the sailing boat. She wore her Sunday best, a navy and white polka dot dress, nipped in at the waist, and a neat little hat covered in dark-blue net. Her hair was softly waved, just touching her shoulders. Ralph thought how serene she looked but as he hurried towards the apparition his mother disappeared into the misty sea spray. Oh but he could hear her singing, 'Ave Ma ... Ave Maria ...'

Ralph is full of confusion. He tries to remember if both of his parents are dead. Had he seen them die? Ever since Mannie's arrival Ralph has been struggling with this confusion.

'It was a strange release,' his father whispers in his ear and Ralph jumps in his semi-sleeping state, turns his head slowly around hoping to catch a glimpse of the wandering spirit that shadows him on the island. There is nobody there, no solid human form or incorporeal spirit; there is only the seascape, the huge cliffs, the crashing waves and a few lonely seagulls drifting across the skyline.

'Wh ... Where!' Ralph cries out, and Mannie jumps, half-afraid and half-excited by this utterance of a word.

'I could not cry in that other world,' his father continues. 'God knows I wanted to but it was all rage, hatred and rage.'

Mannie tugs at Ralph's arm. He turns his head and is again reminded of the impulse to reach out. Now his father is behind him; Ralph can feel the warm breath on the back of his neck.

'Reach out,' his father whispers,' gently applying pressure under Ralph's limp arms, 'we are meant to reach out.'

Ralph senses his arms lifting. For a few seconds he feels powerful as he creates a wingspan as great as the dark bird's. He stretches out to Mannie and realises, in an electrifying sense, that this is another body that he touches, that this is the body of a special person – it is the body of his wife.

Mannie senses there is purpose to Ralph's movement. She leans forward and buries her head in his shoulder, an emaciated shoulder that had once been so strong and a secure place to rest her worried head. Mannie wonders now what she ever had to worry about. It should all have been so simple but she had made it complicated, tortuous at times. What did it matter about the baby now, what did anything matter? She just wants Ralph back.

Ruth quietly approaches Mannie, gently urges her that it is time to go.

'Yes, yes,' Mannie answers hurriedly, reluctantly lifting her head.

'Such a strange thing – I felt just now that Ralph had come back to me. I'm sure he understood what I was saying.'

Ruth smiles. Dreams and hopes, she has heard it all before and sometimes when she lies awake at night she thinks that perhaps it is so – that her patients occasionally wake from their enclosed worlds and become one with reality again.

The Light

Ralph retreats into his own world. The white and the pink mass merge and unmerge; the movement makes him spin. And the little grey bird's warbling is becoming a high-pitched scream – it is all too much for him.

Ralph closes up the fissures that are his ears and eyes. He feels himself swooping into a dark landscape, as dark as a starless sky when the moon sleeps. Gone is gravity, the earth's pull – Ralph travels far beyond the universe as we know it.

Ralph I often wonder what it is that makes you hang on. I know what the doctors might say – that your brain cells are virtually all gone, that physical life can take longer to die than mental life. Or some of the more romantically inclined might talk about the human spirit fighting beyond physical decay. Does any of this fit?

I know that there is still life in your eyes and also great anguish. I do believe that you are aware of what is happening to you. This causes me such torment and provides no answers. Do you want to go on or is your mind struggling to be free of a body that is taking too long to die?

It was the same with your father; years and years of a slow, tortuous decline. And your poor mother, so upset all of the time with terrible stories that she brought back from the home. It was awful because nobody had a clue about dementia, back then. I'm sure part of you anguished over whether it was wrong to keep your father alive, but even so you always carried that 'blue card' with you – the one stating that you were a Catholic and agreed to medical intervention, including the administration of fluids to prolong life; if the situation should arise.

I think you believed there is some process involved in dying that we don't fully understand, although your belief must have been pushed to the limit when Tony was ill and refused all intervention; requesting an assisted suicide. What would you say to this dilemma now?

Possibly you'd say that we know so much and yet we know so little. This was always your stance as a scientist, but it won't help Sophia and I if we have to make a decision about tube feeding, and the blue card is no longer in your wallet. I don't know when you removed it. We really should have talked about this. I feel sick and frightened.

Do you still have the memory of the disaster with the Hubble Space Telescope locked away in your mind? By the time the telescope was fixed you didn't quite understand the significance of all those wonderful pictures sent back to earth, of stars and galaxies being born. But before then – when the problem was ongoing, you said that humankind would never discover anything beyond what already lay in our innermost consciousness. I think you meant that we can only ever discover what we already know but have forgotten.

Was this a strange thing for a scientist to believe?

Perhaps – but it gives me strength because I choose to believe that whatever journey you are on there might be some comforting familiarity to be re-discovered – like painting the colours of the Rings of Saturn with knowledge and ease. Remember how you once felt that you would never capture the beauty of those colours?

This is not a problem for Ralph now. It seems to him that he has travelled beyond a certain point – far beyond the parameters of space travel – to a place where an infinite number of colours splash intermittently against the dark canopy. He is at ease with the dark canopy because it is a liberating emptiness. Nothingness is not the state of terror that he had anticipated, but a necessary staging post taking him on to the next part of the journey. Ralph is a voyager and he is seeking one thing – a glimpse of a luminous star that is brighter and bolder than any star that has ever been captured within the magnifying lens of a telescope.

He used to dream about the star as a child; a time when he felt his imagination was able to stretch beyond the confines of being human. This is what he seeks once again as he tumbles and falls with dizzying speed back down the years of his own evolution, unpicking the threads of learning, culture and sophisticated belief. It is only when the last thread has been unpicked that he will be at one with the dark canopy and the luminous star. He will be part of the question that is left begging – he will simply be free.

Mannie walks away. She manages a half-smile at Amy who continues to pull at her grey cardigan. She turns for an instance when she reaches the door, hoping that Ralph will look up, but he is sleeping – his chin gently resting on his chest. The shopping bag doesn't feel any lighter despite unloading the barley water and Mannie decides that it is the reminiscence album that is the problem. She resolves not to bring it again – she cannot bear the weight of it.

Infinite Energy

Ralph stood at the water's edge by the landing platform. The sea was still and clear, a sheet of glass reflecting a pink-tinged sky against which five doves gracefully swooped in perfect formation – their white feathers glinting in the sun's rays. Ralph experienced an ethereal tranquillity.

Then he felt his body lifting – an experience of levitation that had become increasingly familiar. Ralph discovered that he could turn over with ease, as though gently rolling down hills of cloud. He steadied himself face down and gazed upon the scene below. There was a gap in time, possibly only seconds, before a figure disembarked from the sailing vessel. Ralph had a strange sensation that his body was dissolving as he realised the figure was his double and then the thought occurred to him that the doppelganger was merely his physical body. His thoughts were suspended in the sky but his body was below – rapidly disintegrating.

Ralph concentrated hard and attempted to will his mind to return to ground level. The act took energy – amazingly forceful energy, and then it occurred to him, with total clarity, that this was what he had become – infinite energy; he didn't need his body at all.

'At last!' he cried out, knowing that these were the final words he would ever say or need.

Ruth rang me last night at seven o'clock. She had just finished her shift – I could tell that she had been crying. She explained to me that you had been very agitated and that she had sat with you for a while, but then your breathing became laboured and she paged the doctor because she felt worried.

She assured me that the agitation had given way to calm – that you then remained peaceful up until the end. She was so sorry I had not been present – there had not been time to contact any family member. She murmured something about a blessed release – but even so it had happened suddenly – before any of us had expected. She felt bad because a priest was not available.

I had not long been home – had just put the kettle on for a cup of tea. I hadn't even emptied my shopping bag. I felt numb speaking to Ruth, as though the heart had been ripped out of my life.

I emptied the shopping bag of the few bits and pieces I'd taken to the hospital – had forgotten to give Ruth the chocolate orange – her favourite.

I put the reminiscence album back on the bookshelf – gently squeezing it in between the bookend and the long line of books. The shelf looks cluttered – I will clear it one day – I might even paint it a fresh white.

Then I sat quietly for a while and thought what to do with the house and all of the contents, what to keep and what to discard. I tried not to give into the pain. But then I began to think about how everything vanishes eventually, either slowly – painfully and punishingly slowly – or rapidly, with burning intensity – a life blown away in seconds.

The phone rang and I held back the tears – because it was Sophia – and before I could say anything she told me she was expecting a baby.

Afterwards

September 2008
<u>Kerry Hughes</u>   <u>Form 5B</u>

Notes for class debate: Last week in general science we began to learn about cosmology (big subject!) and Mr Hoyles showed us a 'You Tube' video about the Large Hadron Collider. The video was called 'Large Hadron Rap' and it was a cool introduction to subjects that we won't cover in depth 'til much later – like particle physics, protons, LCH acceleration, dark matter and anti-matter, black holes and the Higgs boson. I had to watch the video loads of times to make that list but I practiced my rap dancing at the same time!

I wish my grandfather Ralph Drew were here to help me with this debate. My grandfather was a cosmologist and talented artist, whose work was cut short by early onset dementia. He died in 1999. I was just seven at the time so my recollections of him are fuzzy, but my mum and grandmother made sure that I never forgot him and have filled in some of the gaps.

My mum didn't inherit my grandfather's interest in science but the artistic bent came through. She is a folk/rock singer, but jokes about never giving up the daytime job – which is why she is our very own school secretary! When we visited my grandmother, after my grandfather died, I began to get curious about his observatory, which was set up in the attic. As I got older my dad helped me to use my grandfather's telescope and other equipment, so I've been really lucky to learn about astronomy from an early age.

Ok – here comes the science bit. These are exciting times for physicists as CERN, the European nuclear research organisation, is about to launch the Large Hadron Collider experiment. As we saw in the video, CERN hopes to find information on the composition of dark matter, which would have excited my grandfather no end as he spent most of his life exploring this stuff.

The rap video shows how The Collider will accelerate particles around a 27km ring and smash them together so close to the speed of light that it will re-create conditions a trillionth of a second after the big bang. This may answer questions such as; what is mass, and what is the 96% of the universe we can't see made of?

A newspaper article stated that the annual UK budget for CERN is £78m plus £512m towards building the Collider since 1995. A lot of money!

My grandfather died because of dementia – a medical condition that kills off a person's brain cells and makes them really confused. Lots of us are going to have it when we get older and some people, like my grandfather, become unwell when they're only in their fifties or sixties. The government puts very little money into medical research and all the major illnesses rely on charities to raise funding. My mum does an annual gig to raise money for Alzheimer's research.

My grandfather worried about what the planet held for future generations. I would have liked to ask him if he believed there is any real benefit, to the human race, in knowing what happened a trillionth of a second after the big bang – or would it not be better to put the money into medical research?

Possible title for debate: Would the millions of pounds spent on scientific research be better put into medical research – which is of benefit to more people?

From:manniedr@googlemail.com
Date: 20 09 2008
To: kerryh@yahoo.co.uk
Subject: Re: form debate

Dear Kerry, thank you for emailing the notes for your class debate to me. So what did your classmates decide – it's a tricky one isn't it?

I'm sure your grandfather would have been excited by the CERN experiment and might have argued that future progress in medicine and other areas often comes unexpectedly from seemingly obscure scientific enquiry – but perhaps not so with the Collider?

In the newspapers the Collider is being referred to as 'The God machine'. This is where your grandfather might suggest we are getting beyond ourselves. I think I'm right in saying that we can't get to the moment of the big bang and we can't really imagine the trillionth of a second before it – as time and space are presumed not to exist before the birth of the universe. This is a mystery don't you think – something I find it hard to get my thoughts around. I wish your grandfather were here to explain it better – he would be so very proud that you are following in his footsteps.

So – the experimenters will have to settle with knowing what happened a trillionth of a second after the big bang – or not. I think it might have pleased your grandfather to know that the end result might be 'back to the drawing board' regarding all our theories.

I am settling in at the retirement village. I should have done this earlier, but I found it hard to think about leaving Grange Farm after your grandfather's death. I am glad I stayed for a few more years; because of all the lovely times I spent there with you and your brother and it was such a pleasure seeing you become interested in your grandfather's observatory.

How is Toby by the way – does he like his new school? There are some lovely big conker trees in the grounds here, so I think he will enjoy it when he comes to visit.

Did I tell you I have started to teach computer classes? I have you to thank for that, encouraging me to keep up with things.

Thank you for the link to the rap video, what fun learning can be these days – nothing like the dreary science lessons we had at school!

Well, that's all for now. Give my love to your mum and dad,

Lots of love, Grandma x

Acknowledgements

In the absence of a mainstream publisher and access to an editor one relies upon the generosity of friends. In this regard I have been fortunate.

The manuscript was first read by Barry Letts*, whose scrupulous attention to detail helped me to step outside of my own perceptions – in order to critique. I must also thank Pam Smith for her detailed response.

Bev Shember, Fran Poston, Rachel Featherstone, Tony Petch, Andy Fletcher, Emma Owens, Pete Thornley, Françoise Watson, Eileen Harrisson and Julie Hirons – thank you for reading the novel pre-publication, insightful comments and proofreading.

Cosmologists and physicists are thin on the ground in the friends' department so I have relied heavily on textual research. The works of Paul Davies proved invaluable in my reflections upon the possibility of building a bridge between physics and metaphysics. I would enthusiastically recommend Marcus Chown to anyone who is seeking an entertaining and accessible route into quantum theory. Richard Panek's 'Seeing and Believing' delivers both history and poetry in its recording of the history of the telescope.

*Barry Letts, actor, director and TV producer, sadly died 12 October 2009. His autobiography *Who and Me* is due to be published December 2009.

Last, but not least, I must thank my partner and best friend Bernie Burns, for providing a nurturing environment (through a great deal of emotional and physical care and support) making it possible for me to write, and eventually finish this work, through long years of illness.

Lightning Source UK Ltd.
Milton Keynes UK
13 December 2009

147455UK00001B/4/P